The Ways of Life by Margaret Oliphant

Two Lives

Margaret Oliphant Wilson was born on April 4th, 1828 to Francis W. Wilson, a clerk, and Margaret Oliphant, at Wallyford, near Musselburgh, East Lothian.

Her youth was spent in establishing a writing style and by 1849 she had her first novel published: Passages in the Life of Mrs. Margaret Maitland.

Two years later, in 1851 Caleb Field was published and also an invitation to contribute to Blackwood's Magazine; the beginning of a life time business relationship.

In May 1852, Margaret married her cousin, Frank Wilson Oliphant. Their marriage produced six children but, tragically, three died in infancy. When her husband developed signs of the dreaded consumption (tuberculosis) they moved to Florence, and then to Rome where, sadly, he died.

Margaret was naturally devastated but was also now left without support and only her income from writing to support the family. She returned to England and took up the burden of supporting her three remaining children by her literary activity.

Her incredible and prolific work rate increased both her commercial reputation and the size of her reading audience. Tragedy struck again in January 1864 when her only remaining daughter Maggie died.

In 1866 she settled at Windsor to be closer to her sons, who were being educated at near-by Eton School.

For more than thirty years she pursued a varied literary career but family life continued to bring problems. Cyril Francis, her eldest son, died in 1890. The younger son, Francis, who she nicknamed 'Cecco', died in 1894.

With the last of her children now lost to her, she had little further interest in life. Her health steadily and inexorably declined.

Margaret Oliphant Wilson Oliphant died at the age of 69 in Wimbledon on 20th June 1897. She is buried in Eton beside her sons.

Index of Contents

A PREFACE - ON THE EBB TIDE

I do not pretend to say that the two stories included in this volume are conscious or intentional studies of the phase of human experience which I can describe in no other way than by calling it the ebb, in contradistinction to that tide in the affairs of men which we all know is, to those who can identify and seize it, the great turning-point of life, and leads on to fortune. But they were at least produced under the influence of the strange discovery which a man makes when he finds himself carried away by the retiring waters, no longer coming in upon the top of the wave, but going out. This does not necessarily mean the decline of life, the approach of age, or any natural crisis, but something more poignant—the wonderful and overwhelming revelation which one time or other comes to most people, that their career, whatever it may have been, has come to a stop: that such successes as they may have achieved are over, and that henceforward they must accustom themselves to the thought of going out with the tide. It is a very startling discovery to one who has perhaps been going with a tolerably full sail, without any consciousness of weakened energies or failing power; and it usually is as sudden as it is strange, a thing unforeseen by the sufferer himself, though probably other people have already found it out, and traced the steps of its approach. Writers of fiction, and those whose work it is to realise and exhibit, as far as in them lies, the vicissitudes and alterations of life, are more usually employed in illustrating the advance of that tide—in showing how it is caught or lost, and with what an impetus, and what accompaniments it flings itself higher and higher up upon the beach, with the sunshine triumphant in the whirl of the big wave as it turns over and breaks into foam, and the flood claps its hands with a rejoicing noise. But yet the ebb has its poetry, too; the colours are more sombre, the sentiment is different. The flood which in its rise seemed almost individual, pervaded by something like conscious life of force and pleasure, becomes like an abstract relentless fate when it pours back into the deep gulf of a sea of forgetfulness, with a rush of whitened pebbles dragged from the beach, or a long expanse of uncovered sands left bare, studded with slippery fragments of rock and the bones of shipwrecked boats. These are no more than symbols of the rising and falling again of human feeling, which, in all its phases, is of the highest interest to those who recognise, even in its imaginary developments, a shadow of their own.

The moment when we first perceive that our individual tide has turned is one which few persons will find it possible to forget. We look on with a piteous surprise to see our little triumphs, our not-little hopes, the future we had still believed in, the past in which we thought our name and fame would still be to the good, whatever happened, all floating out to sea to be lost there, out of sight of men. In the morning all might seem as sure to go on for ever—that is, for our time, which means the same thing—as the sky over us, or the earth beneath our feet; but before evening there was a different story, and the tide was in full retreat, carrying with it both convictions of the past and hope in the future, not only our little laurels, all tossed and withered, and our little projects, but also the very heart of exertion, our confidence in ourselves and providence. The discovery comes in many different ways—in the unresponsive silence which greets an orator who once was interrupted by perpetual cheers, in the publishing of a book which drops and is never heard of more, or, as in the present case, the unsold pictures: and in the changed accent with which the fickle public pronounces a once favoured name.

There are some who salute this discovery with outcries of indignation and refusal to believe. They think, like the French, that they are betrayed, or, like many of us, that an enemy has done this: a malignant critic perhaps, an ill-disposed publisher or dealer: and save their own pride by putting forth explanations, and persuading themselves, if nobody else, that the thing is temporary and an accident, or else that it is due to cruel fate, and the machinations of evil-hearted men. But when, amid the gifts of the artist, be they small or great, he happens to retain the clearer reason, the common-sense of ordinary intelligence, it is more difficult to take refuge in such self-deceptions, merciful expedients of Nature as they may be to blind us to our own misfortunes. The reasonable man has the worst of it in such cases. It is less possible for him to believe in a mysterious fate or in malign influences. He is obliged to allow to himself that the going out of the tide is as natural as its coming in, and that he is no way exempted from the operation of those laws which affect human reputation and comfort as much as the rising and the falling affect the winds and the seas.

These problems of the common life, though they are perhaps less cheerful, are surely as fit subjects for fiction as are the easier difficulties of youth. It is common to say that all the stories have been told and every complication exhausted, so that we can do nothing but repeat the old themes over again, with such variety of treatment as our halting genius can suggest. Romance itself, they say, is gone, which is an assertion strenuously contradicted by the most powerful of our young writers, Mr. Rudyard Kipling, who replies to it in very energetic tones, that, Here is a steam-engine, which is Romance incarnate, the great poetry of form and purpose, a creation, as distinct as Hamlet or Lear, a big, dutiful, but exigent giant which a touch can turn into a destroyer, but loving guidance into the most useful servant and friend of man. The tramp of its mighty feet across the wastes of the sea, bringing the man home to his wife, the son to his mother, is poetry, is joy to this eager spirit. I am disposed in moderation to accept the belief of the young author who has a most broad and manful perception of life as something more than love-making, and to acknowledge the mysterious monstrous thing which he makes heroic. To show in his masterful way how every consenting part of the big machine as it clanks on with large unwieldy steps, so many beats to a minute, sounds a note in the symphony of life and service, a voice in the great strain of song which rises from earth to heaven, is more worthy than all the unsavoury romances of all the decadents. Would not St. Francis, had he lived to see it, have called to Brother Iron and Brother Steel, strong henchmen of God, and Sister Steam, with her wreaths of snow, though her voice be not sweet, to join the song of the Creatures in honour of the Maker, as he called upon fire and water in his famous hymn? or that older minstrel in the ancient ages, to whom "snow and vapour, wind and storms fulfilling His word," were already members of the great choir? It must be added, however, when all is said, that it is the grimy engineer behind watching every valve and guiding every stroke who makes the romance of the machine, as interesting in his way as Romeo, who, though he is the perennial hero, and attracts the greatest general interest, is not so much of a man.

I have often felt while sick or sorry, and craving a little rational entertainment and distraction—which, in my opinion, it is one of the highest aims of the novelist to supply—that the everlasting treatment of the primary problem of youth, as if there was no other in the world, was at once fatiguing to the reader and injudicious on the part of the writer. When we want to be taken out of ourselves by the lively presentment of other people's difficulties and troubles, it is tiresome to be always turned back to the disappointments or the successes of eighteen, or—in deference to the different standard of age held to be interesting by this generation—let us say five-and-twenty. I do not in the least deny the great advantages of that episode in life for treatment in fiction. It is almost the only episode which comes to a distinct, while it may be, at the same time, a cheerful, end; and its popularity is obvious: and it is a subject which women, who form the bulk of readers of fiction, are rarely tired of; all of which points are important. The elder writers made it the chief thread in the web of fancy, but surrounded the young people with plenty of fathers and mothers, neighbours and servants, doctors, clergymen, lawyers, etc., and all the paraphernalia of common life. But I weary of the two by themselves, or almost by themselves, as happens so often; and if the artifices, with which we are so familiar, by which they are brought together, are fatiguing, how much more so are those uglier artifices by which, being linked together, they are torn asunder again, and a fierce duel of what is called passion is set before us against the lurid skies as the chief object of interest in the world? Novelists make a great moan when they are hindered in the working out of such subjects, and cry loudly to heaven and earth against the limited intelligences which object to them, the British matron, the young person, and so forth. It seems to me that they would be more reasonable if they complained of the monotonous demand for a love-story which crushes out of court all the rest of life—so infinite in variety, so full of complication, so humorous, so mysterious, so natural and true.

I have wondered often whether Macaulay and Darwin, and such great men, whom it is the pride of the novel writer to quote as finding their recreation in novels, were not of my opinion; though it is sadly disconcerting to find from his own account that all Mr. Darwin wanted was a story which ended happily—a judgment which is humbling to one's pride in a reader of whom one was so much inclined to boast. So do I like a story which ends happily. And since the public is fond of such small revelations, I may here confess that I have often begun a story with the determination to be high-minded—to treat my young lovers without indulgence, and either kill them or part them in deference to the rules of Art. But my heart has generally failed me, and I have rarely found courage to do them any harm. They will have plenty of trouble in the world, one knows—why should one cross them in the beginning of their career?

These, however, are questions of a lighter mood than the one with which I began, and a manifest digression from that theme. The two stories which follow treat not of the joy and pride of life, but of those so often unforeseen misfortunes and accidents which shape it towards its end. Life appears under a very different aspect to the man who has felt the turn of the tide. Probably the discovery has been quite sudden, startling, and, so far as he knows, private to himself. His friends all the time may go on hailing him as poet, creator—all manner of fine things. If he discloses his discovery to them, he is met by reproaches for his dejection, his distrust and gloomy views; the compliments which he knows so well and believes so little are heaped again upon him; he is out of health, out of spirits, overworked, they say, in want of rest; a few weeks leisure and repose, and he will be himself again—as if it were a mood or a freak of temper, and not a fact staring him in the face. But usually he is too much stunned to speak. He is not dying, or like to die, though his career has come or is coming to an end. It would be far more appropriate, far more dramatic if he were; but death is illogical, and will seldom come at the moment when it is wanted, when it would most appropriately solve the problem of what is to be done after?—which becomes the most pressing, the most necessary of questions. Why did not Napoleon die at Waterloo? He lived to add a pitiful postscript to his existence, to accumulate all kinds of squalid miseries about his end, instead of the dramatic and clear-cut conclusion which he might have attained by a merciful bullet or the thrust of a bayonet. And how well it would be to end thus when we have discovered that our day is over! But so far from that, the man has to go on, as if nothing had happened, "in a cheerful despair," as I have read in a note-book—as if to-day were as yesterday, or perhaps more abundant.

"We poets in our youth, begin in gladness,
But after comes in the end despondency and madness,"

says Wordsworth. "We have wrought no deliverance in the earth," says with profounder meaning a much older poet. A man in such straits may sometimes save himself as Hamlet would have done, with a bare bodkin, had not the thought of that something after death which might be worse even than present calamity deterred him; but if he is of other mettle and cannot run away, or leave his post save at the lawful summons, the question, What he is to do? is overwhelming. No hope of being carried to any island valley of Avillion by stately queens in that boat which is going out with the tide. And no rebellion against fate will do him the slightest service. He has to hold his footing somehow—but how?

I confess that I have not had the courage to follow this question, in either of the cases treated here, to such depths of human discomfiture as may have been, or may yet be. A greater artist might have done so, and led the defeated man through all the depths of humiliation and dismay; but my hand is not strong or firm enough to trace out to the bounds of the catastrophe the last possibilities of the broken career. What in the jargon of the age is called the psychological moment is that in which the first discovery is made, and the startled victim suddenly perceives what has happened to him, and feels in every plank of his boat the downward drag of the ebb tide, and looks about him wildly to see if there is anything he can lay hold of to arrest it, any deliverance or any escape. This is the case of Mr. Sandford, the hero of the first of the following tales: and of many others who are not favoured by so speedy and so complete an answer to this bewildering problem of life.

The other story is different; for Robert Dalyell, the subject of that, has laid his plans arbitrarily to escape out of it, doing what seems to him the best he can for those who belonged to him. And here again there is much more to say than has been said; for the condition of the man who blots himself out of life without dying, and accepts a kind of moral annihilation while yet all the sources of life are warm within him, might well afford us one of the most tragic chapters of human history. But I have shrunk from those darker colours with a compunction for him whom I have made to suffer, which is quite fantastical and out of reason, but yet true. To have brought him into the world for the mere purpose of exhibiting his torments seems bad enough without searching into the depths of them, and betraying those secrets which he himself accepts with a robust commonplace of endurance as the natural consequences of the step he has taken.

I may add here that the circumstances of this latter story, which a just but severe writer has upbraided me with taking from real life, are indeed, so far as the central incident goes, facts in a family history, but facts of which I know neither the date nor the personages involved, all of whom are purely imaginary, as are most of the consequences that follow, at least so far as is known to me.

The reader, I hope, will forgive a writer very little given to explanations, or to any personal appearance, for these prefatory words.

M. O. W. O.

CHAPTER I

He was a man approaching sixty, but in perfect health, and with no painful physical reminders that he had already accomplished the greater part of life's journey. He was a successful man, who had attained at a comparatively early age the heights of his profession, and gained a name for himself. No painter in England was better or more favourably known. He had never been emphatically the fashion, or made one of those great "hits" which are far from being invariably any test of genius; but his pictures had always been looked for with pleasure, and attracted a large and very even share of popular approbation. From year to year, for what was really a very long time, though in his good health and cheerful occupation the progress of time had never forced itself upon him unduly, he had gone on doing very well, getting both praise and pudding—good prices, constant commissions, and a great deal of agreeable applause. A course of gentle uninterrupted success of this description has a curiously tranquillising effect upon the mind. It did not seem to Mr. Sandford, or his wife, or any of his belongings, that it could ever fail. His income was more like an official income, coming in at slightly irregular intervals, and with variations of amount, but wonderfully equal at the year's end, than the precarious revenues of an artist. And this fact lulled him into security in respect to his pecuniary means. He had a very pleasant, ample, agreeable life—a pretty and comfortable house, full of desirable things; a pleasant, gay, not very profitable, but pleasant family; and the agreeable atmosphere of applause and public interest which gave a touch of perfection to all the other good things. He had the consciousness of being pointed out in every assembly as somebody worth looking at: "That's Sandford, you know, the painter." He did not dislike it himself, and Mrs. Sandford liked it very much. Altogether it would have been difficult to find a more pleasant and delightful career.

His wife had been the truest companion and helpmeet of all his early life. She had made their small means do in the beginning when money was not plentiful. She had managed to do him credit in all the many appearances in society which a rising painter finds to his advantage, while still spending very little on herself or her dress. She had kept all going, and saved him from a thousand anxieties and cares. She had sat to him when models proved expensive so often that it was a common joke to say that some reflection of Mrs. Sandford's face was in all his pictures, from Joan of Arc to Queen Elizabeth. Now that the children were grown up, perhaps the parents were a little less together than of old. She had her daughters to look after, who were asked out a great deal, and very anxious to be fashionable and to keep up with their fine friends. The two grown-up girls were both pretty, animated, and pleasant creatures, full of the chatter of society, yet likewise full of better things. There were also two grown-up sons: one a young barrister, briefless, and fond of society too; the other one of those agreeable do-nothings who are more prevalent nowadays than ever before, a very clever fellow, who had just not succeeded as he ought at the University or elsewhere, but had plenty of brains for anything, and only wanted the opportunity to distinguish himself. They were all full of faculty, both boys and girls, but all took a good deal out of the family stores without bringing anything in. Ever since these children grew up the family life had been on a very easy, ample scale. There was never any appearance of want of money, nor was the question ever discussed with the young ones, who had really no way of knowing that there was anything precarious in that well-established family income which provided them with everything they could desire. Sometimes, indeed, Mrs. Sandford would shake her head and declare that she "could not afford" some particular luxury. "Oh, nonsense, mamma!" the girls would say, while Harry would add, "That's mother's rôle, we all know. If she did not say so she would not be acting up to her part." They took it in this way, with the same, or perhaps even a greater composure than if Mr. Sandford's revenues had been drawn from the three per cents.

It was only after this position had been attained that any anxieties arose. At first it had seemed quite certain that Jack would speedily distinguish himself at the bar, and become Lord Chancellor in course of time; and that something would turn up for Harry—most likely a Government appointment, which so well known a man as his father had a right to expect. And Mrs. Sandford, with a sigh, had looked forward with certainty to the early marriage of her girls. But some years had now passed since Ada, who was the youngest, had been introduced, and as yet nothing of that kind had happened. Harry was pleasantly about the world, a great help in accompanying his sisters when Mrs. Sandford did not want to go out, but no appointment had fallen in his way; and the briefs which Jack had procured were very few and very trifling. Things went on quite pleasantly all the same. The young people enjoyed themselves very much—they were asked everywhere. Lizzie, who had a beautiful voice, was an acquisition wherever she went, and helped her sister and her brothers, who could all make themselves agreeable. The life of the household flowed on in the pleasantest way imaginable; everything was bright, delightful, easy. Mrs. Sandford was so good a manager that all domestic arrangements went as on velvet. She was never put out if two or three people appeared unexpectedly to lunch. An impromptu dinner party even, though it might disturb cook, never disturbed mamma. There was no extravagance, but everything delightfully liberal and full. The first vague uneasiness that crept into the atmosphere was about the boys. It was Mrs. Sandford herself who began this. "Did you speak to Lord Okeham about Harry?" she said to her husband one day, when she had been particularly elated by the appearance of that nobleman at her tea-table. He had come to look at a picture, and he was very willing afterwards, it appeared, to come into the drawing-room to tea.

"How could I? I scarcely know him. It is difficult enough to ask a friend—but a man I have only seen twice—"

"Your money or your life," said Harry, with a laugh. He was himself quite tranquil about his appointment, never doubting that some day it would turn up.

"It is easier to ask a stranger than a friend," said Mrs. Sandford. "It is like trading on friendship with a man you know; but this man's nothing but a patron, or an admirer. I should have asked him like—I mean at once."

"Mother was going to say like a shot—she is getting dreadfully slangy, worse than any of us. Let's hope old Okeham will come back; there's not much time lost," said the cheerful youth.

"When your father was your age he was making a good deal of money. We were beginning to see our way," said Mrs. Sandford, shaking her head.

"What an awfully imprudent pair you must have been to marry so early!" cried Jack.

"I wonder what you would say to us if we suggested anything of the kind?" said Miss Ada, who had made herself very agreeable to Lord Okeham.

"A poor painter!" said Lizzie, with a tone in her voice which her mother understood—for, indeed Mrs. Sandford did not at all encourage the attentions of poor painters, having still that early certainty of great matches in her mind.

The young people were quite fond of their parents, very proud of their father, dutiful as far as was consistent with the traditions of their generation: but naturally they were of opinion that fathers and mothers were slightly antiquated, and did not possess the last lights.

"The young ones are too many for you, Mary," said Mr. Sandford; but he added, "It's true what your mother says; you oughtn't to be about so much as you are, doing nothing. You ought to grind as long as you're young—"

"At what, sir?" said Harry, with mock reverence. Mr. Sandford did not reply, for indeed he could not. Instead of giving an answer he went back to the studio, which indeed he had begun to find a pleasant refuge in the midst of all the flow of youthful talk and laughter, which was not of the kind he had been used to in his youth. Young artists, those poor painters whom Mrs. Sandford held at arms' length, are not perhaps much more sensible than other young men, but they have at least a subject on which any amount of talk is possible, and which their elders can understand. Mr. Sandford was proud of his children, and loved them dearly. Their education, he believed, was much better than his own, and they knew a great deal more on general subjects than he did. But their jargon was not his jargon, and though it seemed very clever and knowing, and even amusing for a while, it soon palled upon him. He went back to his studio and to the picture he was painting, for the daylight was still good. It was the largest of his Academy pictures, and nearly finished. It occurred to him as he stood looking at it critically from a distance, with his head on one side and his hand shading now one part now another, that Lord Okeham, though very complimentary, had not said anything about a desire to possess in his small collection a specimen of such a well-known master as—. He remembered, now, that it was with this desire that his lordship had been supposed to be coming. Daniells, the picture dealer, had said as much. "He wants to come and see what you've got on the stocks. Tell you w'at, old man, 'e's as rich as Cressus. Lay it on thick, 'e won't mind—give you two thou' as easy as five 'undred." This was what, with his usual elegant familiarity, Mr. Daniells had said. It occurred to Mr. Sandford, with a curious little pang of surprise, that Lord Okeham had not said a word on the subject. He had admired everything, he had lingered upon some of the smaller sketches, making little remarks in the way of criticism now and then which the painter recognised as very judicious, but he had not said a word about enriching his collection with a specimen, &c. The surprise with which Mr. Sandford noticed this had a sort of sting in it—a prick like the barb of a fish-hook, like the thorn upon a rose. He did not at the moment exactly perceive why he should have felt it so. After a little while, indeed, he began to smile at the idea that it was from Okeham that this sting came. What did one man's favour, even though that man was a cabinet minister, matter to him? It was not that, it was the discussion that followed which had left him with a prick of disquiet, a tingling spot in his mind. He must, he felt, speak to some one about Harry—not Lord Okeham, whom he did not know, who had evidently changed his mind about that specimen of so well-known, &c. He would not dream of saying anything to him, a man not sympathetic, a stranger whom, though he might offer him a cup of tea, he did not really know; but it was very clear that Harry ought to have something to do.

So ought Jack. Jack had a profession, but that did not seem to advance him much. Mr. Sandford had early determined that his sons should not be artists like himself—that they should have no precarious career, dependent on the favour of picture dealers and patrons, notwithstanding that he himself had done very well in that way. He had always resolved from the beginning to give them every advantage. Mr. Sandford recalled to mind that a few years ago he had been very strenuous on this point, talking of the duty of giving his children the very best education, which was the best thing any father could do for his children. He had been very confident indeed on that subject; now he paused and rubbed his chin meditatively with his mahl-stick. Was it possible that he was not quite so sure now? He shook himself free from this troublesome coil of thought, and made up his mind that he must make an effort about Harry. Then he put down his brushes and went out for his afternoon walk.

In earlier days Mrs. Sandford would have come into the studio; she would have talked Lord Okeham over. She would have said, "Oh, he did not like that forest bit, didn't he? Upon my word! I suppose my lord thinks he is a judge!"

"What he said was reasonable enough. He does know something about it. I told you myself I was not satisfied with the balance of colour. The shadow's too dark. The middle distance—"

"Oh, Edward, don't talk nonsense: that's just like you—you're so ridiculously modest. If the cook were to come in one morning and tell you she thought your composition bad, you would say she approached the picture without any bias, and probably what she said was quite true. Come out for a walk."

This, be it clearly understood, was an imaginary conversation. It did not take place for the excellent reason that Mrs. Sandford was in the drawing-room, smiling at the witticisms of her young ones, and saying at intervals, "Come, come, Lizzie!" and "Don't be so satirical, Jack." They were not nearly such good company as her husband, nor did they want her half so much, but she thought they did, and that it was her duty to be there. So Mr. Sandford, who did not think of it at all as a grievance, but only as a natural necessity, had nothing but an imaginary talk which did not relieve him much, and went out for his walk by himself.

It would be foolish to date absolutely from that day a slight change that began to work in him—but it did come on about this time: and that was an anxiety that the boys should get on and begin their life's work in earnest which had not affected him before. He had been too busy to think much except about his work so long as the young ones were well; and the period at which the young ones become men and women is not always easy for a father to discern so long as they are all under his roof as in their childish days. He, too, had let things flow along in the well-being of the time without pausing to inquire how long it was to last, or what was to come of it. A man of sixty who is in perfectly good health does not feel himself to be old, nor think it necessary to consider the approaching end of his career. Something, however, aroused him now about these boys. He got a little irritable when he saw Harry about, playing tennis with the girls, sometimes spending the whole day in flannels. "Why can't he do something?" he said to his wife.

"Dear Edward," said Mrs. Sandford, "what can the poor boy do? He is only too anxious to do something. He is always talking to me about it. If only Lord Okeham or some one would get a post for him. Is there no one you can speak to about poor Harry?"

This was turning the tables upon Harry's father, who, to tell the truth, was very slow to ask favours, and did not like it all. He did speak, however—not to Lord Okeham, but to an inferior potentate, and was told that all the lists were full, although everybody would be delighted, of course, to serve him if possible; and nothing came of that. Then there was Jack. The young man came into dinner one day in the highest spirits. He had got a brief—a real brief—a curiosity which he regarded with a jocular admiration. "I shall be a rich man in no time," he said.

"How much is your fee?" asked one of the girls. "You must take us somewhere with it Jack."

"It is two guineas," Jack said, and then there was a general burst of laughter—that laughter young and fresh which is sweet to the ears of fathers and mothers.

"That's majestic," Harry said; "lend us something, old fellow, for luck," and they all laughed again. They thought it a capital joke that Jack should earn two guineas in six months. It did not hurt him or any of them; he had everything he wanted as if he had been earning hundreds. But Mr. Sandford did not laugh. This time it vexed and disturbed him to hear all the cheerful banter and talk about Jack's two guineas.

"It is all very well to laugh," he said to his wife afterwards, "but how is he ever to live upon that?"

"Dear Edward, it's not like you to take their fun in earnest," said the mother. "The poor boy has such spirits—and then it's always a beginning."

"I am afraid his spirits are too good. If he would only take life a little more seriously—"

"Why should he?" said Mrs. Sandford, taking high ground; "it is his happiest time. If he wanted to marry and set up for himself it might be different. But they have no cares—as yet. We ought to be thankful they are all so happy at home. Few young men love their home like our boys. We ought to be very thankful," she repeated with a devout look upon her upturned face. It took the words out of his mouth. He could not say any more.

But he kept on thinking. The time was passing away with great rapidity—far more quickly than it had ever done. Sunday trod on the heels of Sunday, and the months jostled each other as they flew along. Presently it was Jack's birthday, and there was a dance and a great deal of affectionate pleasure; but when Mr. Sandford remembered how old the boy was, it gave him a shock which none of the others felt. At that age he himself had been Jack's father, he had laid the foundation of his reputation, and was a rising man. If they did not live at home and had not everything provided for them, what would become of these boys? It gave him a sort of panic to think of it. In the very midst of the dance, when he was himself standing in the midst of a little knot of respectable fathers watching the young ones enjoying themselves, this thought overtook him and made him shiver.

"Getting on, I hear, very well at the bar," one of the gentlemen said.

"He is not making very much money as yet," replied Mr. Sandford.

"Oh, nobody does that—at first, at least; but so long as he has you to fall back upon," this good-natured friend said, with a nod of his head.

Mr. Sandford could not make any reply. He kept saying to himself, "Two guineas—two guineas—he could not live very long on that." And Harry had not even two guineas. It fretted him to have this thought come back at all manner of unlikely times. He did not seem able to shake it off. And Mrs. Sandford was always on the defensive, seeing it in his eyes, and making responses to it, speaking at it, always returning to the subject. She dwelt upon the goodness of the boys, and their love of their home, and how good it was for the girls to have them, and how nobody made their mark all at once, "except people that have genius like you," she said with that wifely admiration and faith which is so sweet to a man. What more could he say?

CHAPTER II

About the same time, or a little later, another shadow rose up upon Mr. Sandford's life. It was like the cloud no bigger than a man's hand, like a mere film upon the blue sky at first. Perhaps the very first appearance of it—the faintest shadow of a shade upon the blue—arose on that day when Lord Okeham visited the studio and went away without giving any commission. Not that great personages had not come before with the same result; but that this time there had been supposed to be a distinct purpose in his visit beyond that of taking a cup of tea with the artist's wife and daughters—and this purpose had not been carried out. It was not the cloud, but it was a sort of avant-coureur of the cloud, like the chill little momentary breath which sometimes heralds a storm. No storm followed, but the shadow grew. The next thing that made it really shape itself as a little more than a film was the fact of his Academy picture, the principal one of the year, coming back—without any explanation at all; not purchased, nor even with any application from the print-sellers about an engraving; simply coming back as it had gone into the exhibition. No doubt in the course of a long career such a thing as this, too, had happened before. But there was generally something to account for it, and the picture thus returned seldom dwelt long in the painter's hands. This time, however, it subsided quite quietly into its place, lighting up the studio with a great deal of colour and interest—"a pleasure to see," Mrs. Sandford said, who had often declared that the worst thing of being a painter's wife was that she never liked to see the pictures go away. This might be very true, and it is quite possible that it was a pleasure to behold, standing on its easel against a wall which generally was enlivened only with the earliest of sketches, and against which a lay figure grinned and sprawled.

But the prospect was not quite agreeable to the painter. However cheerfully he went into his studio in the morning, he always grew grave when he came in front of that brilliant canvas. It was the "Black Prince at Limoges," a picture full of life and action, with all the aid of mediæval costume and picturesque groups—such a picture as commanded everybody's interest in Mr. Sandford's younger days. He would go and stand before it for an hour at a time, trying to find some fault in the composition, or in the flesh tints, or the arrangements of the draperies. It took away his thoughts from the subject he was then engaged in working out. Sometimes he would put up his hand to separate one portion from another, sometimes divide it with a screen of paper, sometimes even alter an outline with chalk, or mellow a spot of colour with his brush. There was very little fault to be found with the picture. It carried out all the rules of composition to which the painter had been bred. The group of women which formed the central light was full of beauty; the sick warrior to whom they appealed was a marvel of strength and ferocity, made all the keener by the pallor of his illness. There was nothing to be said against the picture; except, perhaps, that, had not this been Mr. Sandford's profession, there was no occasion for its existence at all.

When the mind has once been filled with a new idea it is astounding how many events occur to heighten it. Other distinguished visitors came to the studio, like Lord Okeham, and went away again, having left a great deal of praise and a little criticism, but nothing else, behind them. These were not, perhaps, of importance enough to have produced much effect at an ordinary moment, but they added to the general discouragement. Mr. Sandford smiled within himself at the mistakes the amateurs made, and the small amount of real knowledge which they showed; but when they were gone the smile became something like that which is generally and vulgarly described as being on the wrong side of the mouth. It was all very well to smile at the amateurs—but it was in the long run their taste, and not that of the heaven-born artist, which carried the day; and when a man takes away in his pocket the sum which ought to supply your balance at your banker's, the sight of his back as he goes out at the door is not pleasant. Mr. Sandford had not come to that pitch yet; but he laughed no longer, and felt a certain ruefulness in his own look when one after another departed without a word of a commission. There were other things, too, not really of the slightest importance, which deepened the impression—the chatter of Jack's friends, for instance, some of whom were young journalists, and talked the familiar jargon of critics. He came into the drawing-room one day during one of his wife's teas, and found two or three young men, sprawling about with legs stretched out over the limited space, who were pulling to pieces a recent exhibition of the works of a Royal Academician. "You would think you had got among half a dozen different sorts of people dressed for private theatricals," said one of the youths. "Old models got up as Shakespearian kings, and that sort of thing. You know, Mrs. Sandford; conventional groups trying to look as if they were historical."

"I remember Mr. White's pictures very well," said Mrs. Sandford. "I used to think them beautiful. We all rushed to see what he had in the exhibition, upon the private view day, when I did not know so much about it as I do now."

"Ah, yes; before you knew so much about it," said the art authority. "You would think very differently to-day."

"The whole school is like that," said another. "Historical painting is gone out like historical novel-writing. The public is tired of costume. Life is too short for that sort of thing. We want a far more profound knowledge of the human figure and beauty in the abstract—"

"Stuff!" said Harry; "the British public doesn't want your nudities, whatever you may think."

"The British public likes babies, and sick girls getting well, and beautiful young gentlemen saying eternal adieux to lovely young ladies," said one of the girls.

"To be sure, that sort of thing always goes on; but everybody must feel that in cultured circles there is a far greater sense of the beauty of colour for itself and art for art than in those ridiculous old days when the subject was everything—"

"You confuse me with your new lights," said Mrs. Sandford. "I always did think there was a great deal in a good subject."

"My dear Mrs. Sandford!" cried one of the young men, laughing; while another added, with the solemnity of his kind—

"People really did think so at one time. It was a genuine belief so long as it lasted. I am not one of those who laugh at faith so naïf. Whatever is true even for a time has a right to be respected," said this profound young man.

Mr. Sandford came in at this point, having paused a little to enjoy the fun, as he said to himself. It was wonderful to hear how they chattered—these babes. "I am glad to hear that you are all so tolerant of the old fogeys," he said, with a laugh as he showed himself. And one at least of the young men had the good taste to jump up as if he were ashamed of himself, and to take his legs out of the way.

"I suppose that's the new creed that those fellows were giving forth," he said to Jack, when the other young men were gone.

"Oh, I don't know, sir," said Jack, with an embarrassed laugh. "We all of us say our say."

"But that is the say of most of you, I suppose," said his father.

"Well, sir, I suppose every generation has its own standard. 'The old order changeth,' don't you know—in art as well as in other things."

"I see; and you think we know precious little about it," said Mr. Sandford, with a joyless smile which curled his lip without obeying any mirthful impulse. He felt angry and unreasonably annoyed at the silly boys who knew so little. "But they know how to put that rubbish into words, and they get it published, and it affects the general opinion," he said to himself, with perhaps a feeling, not unnatural in the circumstances, that he would like to drown those kittens with their miauling about things they knew nothing about. Angry moods, however, did not last long in Mr. Sandford's mind. He went back to his studio and looked at the "Black Prince" in the light of these criticisms. And he found that some of the old courtiers in attendance on the sick warrior did look unfeignedly like old models, which indeed they were, and that there was more composition than life in the attitudes of the women. "I always thought that arm should come like this," he said to himself, taking up his chalk.

One day about this time he had a visit from Daniells, the picture dealer, leading a millionaire—a newly-fledged one—who was making a gallery and buying right and left. Daniells, though he was very dubious about his h's, was a good fellow, and always ready to stand by a friend. He was taking his millionaire a round of the studios, and especially to those in which there was something which had not "come off," according to his phraseology. The millionaire was exceptionally ignorant and outspoken, expressing his own opinion freely. "What sort of a thing have we got here?" he said, walking up to the "Black Prince;" "uncommon nice lot of girls, certainly; but what are they all doing round the fellow out of the hospital? I say, is it something catching?" he cried, giving Mr. Sandford a dig with his elbow. Daniells laughed at this long and loudly, but it was the utmost the painter could do to conjure up a simple smile. He explained as well as he could that they were begging for life, and that the town was being sacked, a terrible event of which his visitor might have heard.

"Sacked," said the millionaire; "you mean that they're factory hands and have got the sack, or that they have been just told they've got to work short time. I understand that; and it shows how human nature's just the same in all ages. But I can tell you that in Lancashire it's a nice rowing he'd have got instead of all these sweet looks. They would not have let him off like that, don't you think it. Wherever you get your women from, ours ain't of that kind."

Sandford tried to explain what kind of a sack it was, but he did not succeed, for the rich man was much pleased with his own view.

"It's a fine picture," said Daniells; "Mr. Sandford, he's one of the very best of our modern masters, sir. He has got a great name, and beautiful his pictures look in a gallery with the others to set 'em off. Hung on the line in the Academy, and collected crowds. I shouldn't 'a been surprised if they'd 'ad to put a rail round it like they did to Mr. Frith's."

He gave a wink at Mr. Sandford as he spoke, which made our poor painter sick.

"I've got one of Frith's," said the millionaire.

"You'll 'ave got one of every modern artist worth counting when you've got Mr. Sandford's," said Daniells, with a pat upon the shoulder to his wealthy client. That gentleman turned round, putting his hands into his pockets.

"I've seen some pictures as I liked better," he said.

"Yes, I know. You've seen that one o' Millais', a regular stunner; but, God bless you, that's but one figger, and twice the money. Look at the work in that," cried the dealer, turning his man round again, who gave the picture another condescending inspection from one corner to the other.

"I don't deny there's a deal of work in it," he said, "if it's painted fair with everything from the life; and I don't mind taking it to complete my collection; but I'll expect to have that considered in the price," he added, turning once more on the painter. "You see, Mr. — (What's the gentleman's name, Daniells?) I am not death on the picture for itself. It's a fine showy picture, and I don't doubt 't'll look well when it's hung; but big things like that, as don't tell their story plain, they're not exactly my taste. However, it's all right since Daniells says so. The only man I know that goes in for that sort of thing thinks all the world of Daniells. 'Go to Daniells,' he says, 'and you'll be all right.' So I'll take the picture, but I'll expect a hundred or two off for ready money. I suppose there's discount in all trades."

"Say fifty off, and you'll do very well, and get a fine thing cheap," said Daniells.

Mr. Sandford's countenance had darkened. He was very amiable, very courteous, much indisposed to bargaining, but he felt as if his customer had jumped upon him, and it was all he could do to contain himself. "I never make—" he began, with a little haughtiness most unusual to him; but before he had said the final words he caught Daniells' eye, who was making anxious signs to him. The picture dealer twisted his face into a great many contortions. He raised his eyebrows, he moved his lips, he made all kinds of gestures; at last, under a pretence of looking at a sketch, he darted between Mr. Sandford and the other, and in a hoarse whisper said "Take it," imperatively, in the painter's ear.

Mr. Sandford came to an astonished pause. He looked at the uncouth patron of art, and at the dealer, and at the picture, in turn. It was on his lips to say that nothing would induce him to let the "Black Prince" go; but something stopped and chilled him—something, he could not tell what. He paused a moment, then retired suddenly to the back of the studio. "I'm not good at making bargains—I will leave myself," he said, "in Mr. Daniells' hands."

"Ah, a bad system—a bad system. Every man ought to make his own bargains," said the rich man.

Mr. Sandford did not listen. He began to turn over a portfolio of old sketches as if that were the most important thing in the world. He heard the voices murmur on, sometimes louder, sometimes lower, broken by more than one sharp exclamation, but restrained himself and did not interfere. Many thoughts went through his mind while he stooped over the big portfolio, and turned over, without seeing them, sketch after sketch. Why should he be bidden to "take it" in that imperative way? What did Daniells know which made him interfere with such a high hand? He was tempted again and again to turn round, to put a stop to the negotiation, to say, as he had the best right, "I'll have none of this;" but he did not do it, though he could not even to himself explain why.

He found eventually that Daniells had sold the picture for him at a reduction of fifty guineas from the original price, which was a thing of no importance. He hated the bargain, but the little sacrifice of the money moved him not at all. He recovered his temper or his composure when the arrangement was completed, and smiled with a reserved acceptance of the millionaire's invitation to "come to my place and see it hung," as he showed the pair away. They were a well-matched pair, and Daniells was no doubt far better adapted to deal with each a man than a sensitive, proud artist, who did not like to have his toes trodden upon. After a while, indeed, Mr. Sandford felt himself quite able to smile at the incident, and shook off all his annoyance. He went in to luncheon with the cheque in his hand.

"I have sold the 'Black Prince,'" he said, with a certain pleasure, even triumph, in his voice, remembering how Jack's friends had scoffed, if not at the picture, at least at the school to which it belonged.

"Ah!" cried Mrs. Sandford, half pleased, half regretful. "I knew we should not have to give it house-room long." She gave a glance round her as if she had heard something derogatory to the picture too.

"Who have you taken in and done for this time, father?" said Harry, who was given to banter.

"Was it that horrid man who came with Mr. Daniells?" cried Lizzie. "Oh, papa, I should not have thought you would have sold a nice picture to such a man."

"Art-patrons are like gift-horses; we must not look them in the mouth," said the painter. "There are quantities of h's, no doubt, to be found about the studio; but if we stood upon that—"

"So long as he doesn't leave out anything, either h's or 0's, in his cheque."

Mr. Sandford felt slightly, unreasonably offended by any reference to the cheque. He gave it to his wife to send to the bank, with an annoyed apprehension that she would make some remark upon the fifty guineas which were left out. But Mrs. Sandford had not been his wife for thirty years without being able to read the annoyance in his face. And though she did not know what was its cause she respected it, and said not a word about the difference which her quick eye saw at once. Could it be that which had vexed Edward? she asked herself—he was not usually a man who counted his pounds in that way.

The sending off of the "Black Prince," its packing and directing, and all the details of its departure, occupied him for some time. It was August, the beginning of holiday time, when, though never without a protest at the loss of the light days, even a painter idles a little. And the youngest boy had come from school, and they were all going to the seaside. Mr. Sandford did not like the bustle of the moment. He proposed to stay in town for a few days after the family, and join them when they had settled down in their new quarters. Before they went, however, he had an interview with one of those friends of Jack's who were always about the house, and whose opinions on art were so different from Mr. Sandford's, which gave another touch of excitement to the household. The young fellow wanted to marry Lizzie, as had been a long time apparent to everybody but her father. There was nothing to be said against him except that he had not much money; but Mr. Sandford thought that young Moulton looked startled when he had to inform him that Lizzie would have no fortune. "Of course that was not of the least consequence," he said, but he gave his future father-in-law a curious and startled look.

"I think he was disappointed that there was no money," the painter said afterwards to his wife.

"Oh, Edward! there is nothing mercenary about him!" said Mrs. Sandford; but she sighed and added, "If there only had been a little for her—just enough for her clothes. It makes such a difference to a young married woman. It is hard to have to ask your husband for everything."

"Did you think so, Mary?" he asked, with a smile but a sense of pain.

"I—but we were not like ordinary people, we were just two fools together," said the wife, with a smile which brightened all her face; "but," she added, shaking her head, "we don't marry our daughters like that."

"If she is half as good to him as you have been to me—"

"Oh, don't speak," she said, putting up her hand to stop his mouth. "Lance Moulton can never be the hundredth part so good as my husband." But she stopped after this little outburst, and laughed, and again shaking her head, repeated, "But we don't marry our daughters like that."

He felt inclined to ask, but did not, why?

When they all went away Mr. Sandford felt a little lonely, left by himself in the house, and perhaps it was that as much as anything else that set him thinking again. His wife had pressed the question of what Lizzie would want if she married young Moulton, who was only a journalist, on several occasions, until at last they had both decided that a small allowance might be made to her in place of a fortune.

"Fifty pounds is the interest of a thousand, and that is what she will have when we die," Mrs. Sandford said, who was not learned in per cents. "I think we might give her fifty pounds a year, Edward."

"Fifty pounds will not do much good," he said.

"Not in their housekeeping, perhaps; but to have even fifty pounds will be a great thing for her. It will make her so much more comfortable." Thus they concluded the matter between them, though not without a certain hesitation on Mr. Sandford's part. It was strange that he should hesitate. He had always been so liberal, ready to give. There was no reason why he should take fright now. There was the millionaire's cheque for the "Black Prince," which had just been paid into the bank, leaving a comfortable balance to their credit. There was no pressure of any kind for the moment. To those who had known what it was to await their next payment very anxiously in order to pay very pressing debts, and had seen the little stream of money flowing, flowing away, till it almost seemed to be on the point of disappearing altogether, the ease of having a considerable sum to their credit was indescribable; but Mrs. Sandford was more and more wrapped up in the children, and though never indifferent, yet a little detached in every-day thought and action from her husband. She did not ask him as usual about his commissions and his future work. She seemed altogether at ease in her mind about everything that was not the boys and the girls.

The house was very quiet when they were all away. Merely to look into the drawing-room was enough to give any one a chill. The sense of emptiness where generally every corner was full, and silence where there were always so many voices, was very depressing. Mr. Sandford consoled himself by a very hard day's work the first day of the absence of his family, getting on very well indeed, and making a great advance in the picture he was painting—a small picture intended for one of his oldest friends. In the evening, as he had nothing else to occupy him, he moved about the studio, not going into the other parts of the house at all, and amused himself by making a little study of the moonlight as it came in upon the plants in the conservatory. His house was in a quarter not fashionable, somewhere between St. John's Wood and Regent's Park, and consequently there was more room than is usual in London, a pretty garden and plenty of air. The effect of the moonlight and the black exaggerated shadows amused him. The thought passed through his mind that if perhaps he were one of the newfangled school which Jack's friends believed in, he might turn that unreal scene which was so indubitable a fact into a picture and probably make a great success as an impressionist—an idea at which he smiled with a milder but not less genuine contempt than the young impressionist might have felt for Mr. Sandford's school. He had half a mind to do it—to conceal his name and send it to one of the lesser exhibitions, so as afterwards to have a laugh at the young men, and prove to them how easy the trick was, and that any old fogey who took the trouble could beat them in their own way. Next morning, however, he threw the sketch into a portfolio, with a horror of the black and white extravagance which in the daylight offended his artist-eye, and which he had a suspicion was not so good after all, or so easy a proof of the facility of doing that sort of thing as he had supposed. And that day his work did not advance so quickly or so satisfactorily. He listened for the swing of the door at the other end of the passage which connected the studio with the house, though he knew well enough there was no one who could come to disturb him. There are days when it is so agreeable to be disturbed! And it was when he was painting in this languid way, and, as was natural, not at all pleasing himself with his work, that there suddenly and most distinctly came before him, as if some one had come in and said it, a thing—a fact—which strangely enough he had not even thought of before. When it first occurred to him his hand suddenly stopped work with an action of its own before the mind had time to influence it, and there was a sudden rush of heat to his head. He felt drops of moisture come out on his forehead; his heart for a second paused too. His whole being received a shock—a start. For the first moment he could scarcely make out what this extraordinary sudden commotion, for which his mind seemed only partially responsible, could be.

This was what had in a moment, in the twinkling of an eye, occurred to the painter. He had, of course, been aware of it before without giving any particular importance to the fact. The fact, indeed, in a precarious, uncertain profession like his, in which a piece of good fortune might occur at any moment, was really not of the first importance; but it flashed upon him now in a significance and with a force which no such thing had ever held before. It was this—that when he had completed the little picture upon which he was working he had no other commission of any kind on hand. It sounds very prosaic to be a thing capable of giving such a tragic shot—but it was not prosaic. One can even conceive circumstances in which despair and death might be in such words; and to no one in Mr. Sandford's position could they be pleasant. Even if the fact represented no material loss, it would represent loss—which at his age could never be made up—loss of acceptance, loss of position, that kind of failure which is popularly represented as being "shelved," put aside as a thing that is done with; always a keen and grievous pang. But to our painter the words meant more than that. They meant a cutting off of the ground from under his feet, a sudden arrest of everything, a full stop, which in his fully flowing liberal life was a tragic horror and impossibility, a something far more terrible than death. It had upon him something of the character of a paralytic stroke. His hand, as we have said, stopped work sharply, suddenly; it trembled, and the brush with which he was painting fell from it; his limbs tottered under him, his under lip dropped, his heart gave a leap and then a dead pause. He stumbled backwards for a few steps and sank into a chair.

Well! it was only for a few moments that he remained under the influence of this shock. He picked himself up again, and then picked up his brush and dried the perspiration from his forehead, and his heart with a louder beat went on again as if also crying out "Well!" When he had recovered the power of thought—which was not for a moment or two—he smiled to himself and said, "What then?" Such a thing had happened before. In an artist's life there are often hair-breadth 'scapes, and now and then the most prosperous comes, as it were, to a dead wall—which is always battered through by a little perseverance or else opens by itself, melting asunder at the touch of some heaven-sent patron or happy accident, and so all goes on more prosperously than before. Mr. Sandford had passed through many such crises at the beginning of his career, and even when fully established had never been entirely certain from whence his next year's income was to come. But it had always come; there had never been any real break in it—no failure of the continuity. He had seemed to himself to be as thoroughly justified in reckoning upon this continuity as any man in an office with so much a year. It might be a little more or a little less, and there was always that not unpleasant character of vagueness about it. It might even by a lucky chance for one fortunate year be almost doubled, and this had happened on rare occasions; but very seldom had there been any marked diminution in the yearly incomings. He said, "Pooh, pooh," to himself as he went up to his picture again smiling, with his brush in his hand; not for such a matter as that was he going to be discouraged. It was a thing that had happened before, and would no doubt happen again. He began to work at his picture, and went on with great spirit for perhaps a quarter of an hour, painting in (for he had no model that morning) a piece of drapery from a lay figure, and catching just the tone he wanted on the beautiful bit of brocade which figured in the picture as part of a Venetian lady's majestic dress. He was unusually successful in his work, and also succeeded for ten perhaps of these fifteen minutes in amusing himself and distracting his thoughts from that discovery. A bit of success is very exhilarating; it made him more confident than anything else could have done. But when he had got his effect his smile began to fade away, and his face grew grave again, and his hand trembled once more. After a while he was obliged to give up and take a rest, putting down his palette and brush with a sort of impatience and relief in getting rid of them. Could he have gone straight to his wife and made her take a turn with him in the garden, or even talked it over with her in the studio, no doubt the impression would have died off; but she was absent, and he could not do that; most likely, indeed, if she had been at home she would have been absorbed in some calculation about Lizzie's wedding, and would not have noticed his preoccupation at all.

He sat down again in that chair, and said once more to himself, "What then?" and thought over the times in which this accident had happened before. But there now suddenly occurred to him another thought which was like the chill of an icy hand touching his heart. The same thing had happened before—but he had never been sixty before. He felt himself struck by this as if some one had given him a blow. It was quite true; he had called himself laughingly an old fogey, and when he and his old friends were together they talked a great deal about their age and about the young fellows pushing them from their seats. How much the old fellows mean when they say this, heaven knows. So long as they are strong and well they mean very little. It is an amusing kind of adoption of the folly of the young which seems to show what folly it is—a sort of brag in its way of their own superiority to all such decrepitudes, and easy power of laughing at what does not really touch them. But alone in their own private retirements, when a thought like this suddenly comes, a sharp and sudden realisation of age and what it means, no doubt the effect is different. For the moment Mr. Sandford was appalled by the discovery he had made, which had never entered his mind before. Ah! a pause in one's means of making one's living, a sudden stop in the wheels of one's life, is a little alarming, a little exciting, perhaps a discouragement, perhaps a sharp and keen stimulant at other times: at forty, even at fifty, it may be the latter; but at sixty!—this gives at once a new character to the experience—a character never apprehended before. His heart, which had begun to spring up with an elasticity natural to him, stopped again—nay, did not stop, but fell into a sudden dulness of beating, a subdued silence as if ice-bound. Sensation was too much for thought; his mind could not go into it; he only felt it, with a dumb pang which was deeper than either words or thought.

He could not do any more work that day. He tried again two or three times, but ended by putting down his palette with a sense of incapacity such as he thought he had never felt before. As a matter of fact, he might have felt it a hundred times and attached no importance to it; he would have gone into the house, leaving his studio, and talked or read, or gone out for a walk, or to his club, or to see a friend, saying he did not feel up to work to-day, and there would have been an end of it. But he was alone, and none of these distractions were possible to him. Luncheon came, however, which he could not eat, but sat over drearily, not able to get away from the impression of that thought. Afterwards it occurred to him that he would go and see Daniells and ask him—he was not quite clear what. He could not go to one of his friends and ask, "Am I falling off—do you see it? Has my hand lost its cunning—am I getting old and is my mind going?" He could not ask any one such questions as these. He smiled at it dolefully, feeling all the ridicule of the suggestion. He knew his mind was not going—but—At last he made up his mind what he would do. It was a long walk to Bond Street, but it was now afternoon and getting cooler, and the walk did him good. He reached Daniells' just before the picture dealer left off business for the day. He was showing some one out very obsequiously through the outer room all hung with pictures when he saw Sandford coming in. The stranger looked much interested and pleased when he heard Sandford's name.

"Introduce me, please," he said, "if this is the great Mr. Sandford, Daniells."

"It is, Sir William," said Daniells; and Sir William offered his hand with the greatest effusion. "This is a pleasure that I have long desired," he said.

Mr. Sandford was surprised—he was taken unawares, and the greeting touched his heart. "After all, perhaps it isn't that," he said to himself.

"What a piece of luck that you should have come in just then! Why, that's Sir William Bloomfield—just the very man for you to know."

"Why for me more than another? I know his name, of course," said Mr. Sandford, "and he seems pleasant; but I'm too old for new friends."

"Too old; stuff and nonsense! You're always a-harping on that string. He's just the man for you, just the man," said Daniells, rubbing his hands.

Mr. Sandford was amused—perhaps a little pleased by this encounter; and the pressure of his heavy thoughts was stilled. He began to look at the new pictures which had come into the gallery, to admire some and criticise others. Daniells had the good sense always to listen to Mr. Sandford's criticisms with attention. They had furnished him with a great many telling phrases, and given to his own rough and practical knowledge of art a little occasional polish which surprised and overawed many of his customers. He listened admiringly now as usual.

"What a deal you do know, to be sure!" he said after a while. "I don't know one of them that can make a thing clear like you, old man. It's a shame—" and here he coughed and broke off, as if endeavouring to swallow his last words.

"What is a shame?" The broken sentence changed Mr. Sandford's mood again—the momentary cheer died away. "Daniells," he said, "I want you to tell me what you meant the other day by forcing me to accept that man's offer. Yes, you did. I should not have let him have the picture but for you."

"Forcing him! Oh, that's a nice thing to say—the most obstinate fellow in all London!"

"Never mind that; I can see you are fencing. Come, why did you do it?"

Daniells paused for some time. He said a great many things to stave off his confusion, many half-things which involved others, and made his answer perhaps more clear than if he had put it directly into words.

"I see," Mr. Sandford said at last, "you thought it very unlikely that I should sell it at all to any one who knew better."

"It ain't that. They don't know half enough, hang 'em! or they wouldn't run after a booby like Blank and neglect you."

Mr. Sandford smiled what he felt to be a very sickly smile. "We must let Blank have his day," he said, "I don't grudge it him; but I'd like to know why my chances are so bad. I have always sold my pictures."

Daniells gave him a sudden look, as if he would have spoken; then thought better of it, and said nothing.

"I have had no reason to complain," Mr. Sandford continued; "I have done very well on the whole. I have never had extravagant prices like Em or En."

"No," said Daniells; "you see, you've never made an 'it. You've gone on doing good work, and you've always done good work. I'd say that if I were to die for it; but you've never made an 'it."

"I suppose that's true; but you need not put it so very frankly," said the painter, with a laugh.

"Frankly! I've got occasion to put it frankly; and I say it's a damned shame—that's what it is," cried Daniells, raising his voice.

"You've had occasion? Now that we're on this subject, I should like to get to the bottom of it. You've had occasion?"

"Well, of course," said the picture dealer, "if you drive me into a corner. I'm in the middle of everything, and I hear what people say—"

"What do they say? That I've lost my sense of colour like old Millrain, or fallen into my dotage like—"

"Nonsense, Sandford! You know it's nothing of the kind. Don't talk such confounded nonsense. You are painting quite as well as ever, you know you are. They—people don't care for that sort of thing. It's too good for them, or you're too good for them, or I don't know what."

Mr. Sandford kept smiling—not for pleasure; he was conscious of that sort of fixed smile that might be thought a sneer, at those people for whom he was too good. "And you've had occasion," he said, "to prove this?"

"Don't smile at me like that—don't look like that. If you knew how I've argued and put it all before 'em—I've said a hundred times if I've said once, 'Sandford! why, Sandford's one of the best. There isn't a better educated painter not in England. You can't pick a hole in his pictures, try as you like.'"

"Am I indeed so much discussed?" said the victim. "I did not know I was of such importance. And on what ground have you held this discussion, Daniells? There must have been some occasion for it. I don't see anything here of mine."

"Look here," cried the picture dealer, roused, "if you won't believe me." He opened the door of an inner room, into which Mr. Sandford followed him. And there, with their faces turned to the wall, were three pictures in a row. The shape of them gave him a faint, uneasy feeling. By this time Daniells had been wound up to self-defence, and thought of the painter's feelings no more.

"Look 'ere," he said, "I shouldn't have said a word if you had let well alone—but look 'ere." Before one of the pictures was visible Mr. Sandford knew what he was going to see. Three pictures of his own, of a kind for which he had been famous—cabinet pictures, for which there had always been the readiest market. He recognised them all with a faintness that made his brain swim and the light go from his eyes. They seemed so familiar, like children. At the first glance, without looking at them, he knew what they were and all about them, and had a sick longing that the earth would open and swallow them, and hide his shame, for so it seemed.

"If that don't show how I've trusted you, nothing can," said the dealer. "I thought they were as safe as the bank. I bought them all on spec, thinking I'd get a customer as soon as they were in the shop—and, if you'll believe me, nobody'll have them. I can't tell what people are thinking of, but that's the truth."

Mr. Sandford stood with the light going out of his eyes, gazing straight before him. "In that case—in that case," he began, "you should—I must—"

"I say, don't take it like that, old man. It's the fortune of war. One up and another down. It can't be helped, don't you know. Sandford, I say, why, it'll come all right again in half-a-dozen years or so. It'll come all right after a time."

"What did you say?" said Mr. Sandford, dazed. Then he answered vaguely, "Oh yes; all right—all right."

"What's the matter? I've been a wretched fool. Sandford, here, I say, have a glass of wine."

"There's nothing the matter. It seems to me a little—cold. I know—I know it's not a cold day; but there's a chill wind about, penetrating—thanks, Daniells, you've cleared up my problem very well. Now, I think—I think I understand."

"Don't go now, Sandford; don't go like this."

"I want," he said, smiling again, "to think it over. Much obliged to you, Daniells, for helping me to understand."

"Sandford, don't go like this. You make me awfully anxious—I'm sure you're ill. I can't let you go out of my place, looking so dreadfully ill, without some one with you."

"Some one with me! I hope you don't mean to insult me, Daniells. I am perfectly well—a little startled, but that's all. I shall go and take a walk, and blow away the cobwebs, and—think it over. That's the best thing. I'm much obliged to you, Daniells. Good-bye."

"Have a hansom, at least," Daniells said.

"No hansom," Mr. Sandford answered, turning upon the dealer with a curious smile. He even laughed a little—low, but quite distinct. "No, I'll have no hansom. Good-bye, Daniells, good-bye."

And in a minute he was gone. The picture dealer went out to the door after him, and followed him with his eyes until his figure was lost in the crowd. Daniells was alarmed. He blamed himself for his frankness. "I never thought he'd have taken it to heart like that," he said to himself. "Yes, I did; or I might have done—he's awful proud. But I'm 'asty. I can't help it; I'm always doing things I'm sorry for. Anyhow, he must have found it out some time, sooner or later," the dealer said to himself; and this philosophy silenced his fears.

CHAPTER IV

Mr. Sandford knew nothing till he found himself in the Regent's Park, not far from his house. He had passed through the crowds in the street with his life and thoughts suspended, feeling that to think was impossible, seeing only before him the line of the three pictures standing against the wall. They seemed to accompany him on his way, showing against the front of the houses wherever he turned his eyes. Three pictures, painted cheerfully, without a premonition, or any sense of failure, or a moment's fear that they would ever stand with their faces against a dealer's wall. One of them had been a great favourite with his wife. The youngest girl—little Mary—had sat for one of the figures, and Mrs. Sandford had not wished to let it go. "I wish we could afford to keep this," she said; "it is like selling our own flesh and blood." But most painters have to accustom themselves to that small trouble, and even she had laughed at herself. And now to think that it had never been sold at all—that it was unsaleable, oh, heaven! The sense of a dreadful humiliation, far more than was reasonable, filled the painter's mind. The man whom he had always liked, but partly despised—Daniells, who was as ignorant as a pig, who knew a picture indeed when he saw it, but had not a notion why he liked it, nor could render a reason or tell how he knew one to be bad or another good—that he should be losing by his kindness, should be out of pocket, burdened by three "Sandfords" with their faces against the wall! Mr. Sandford's gentle contempt came back upon him with a shock of humiliation and shame. To sneer at a man who had suffered by him, who had given money for his unsaleable work—a man who had thus shown himself a better man than he: for Daniells had never said a word, probably never would have said a word, listened to the painter's calm assumptions and taken no notice, having it in his power all the time to shame him! Nay, he had done even more than this—he had brought his own customer out of his way, in pity and friendship, to buy that "Black Prince," no doubt equally unsaleable, though—heaven help the poor painter!—he had not found it out. The pang of this humiliation, mingled with tingling shame and a painful gratitude and admiration, quivered through and through him, penetrating the dark dismay and pain of his suspended thoughts.

He began to notice everything more clearly when he got into the park. The August afternoon was softening every moment into the deeper sweetness of the evening. He avoided instinctively the frequented parts, where the children were playing and people walking about, and made a long circuit round the outskirts of the park, where only a rare passenger was to be met with now and then. The air was sweet, though it was the air of town. The leaves were fluttering in a light breeze, the birds singing their evening songs, thrushes repeating a hundred questions, blackbirds unconditional, piping loud and clear, almost as good as nightingales. He was a man who was not hard to please, and even Regent's Park delighted him on a summer evening. He felt it even now, notwithstanding the shadow that was over him. Never, up to this time, had care hung so heavy on Mr. Sandford but what he could escape from it by help of the artist-eye, ever ready to seize a passing effect, or by the gentle heart which was full of sympathy with every human emotion or even whim of passing fancy. His heart was unaccustomed to anything tragical. It tried even now to beguile him and escape; to withdraw his attention to the long, streaming, level rays of the sinking sun; to get him out of himself to the aid of the child who had broken its toy and was crying with such passion—far more than a man can show for losses the most terrible—by the side of the road. And these expedients answered for the moment. But what had befallen him now was not to be eluded as other troubles had been. He could not escape from it. The most ingenious imagination could not lessen it by turning it over and over. Behind the sunset rays a strange vision of the unsold pictures came out into the very sky. They shaped themselves behind the child, whom it was so easy to pacify with a shilling, against the park palings. Three—which was one of the complete numbers, as if to prove the fulness of the disaster—three pictures unsold in Daniells' inner room, and not a commission in hand, nothing wanted from him, no one to buy. After thus trying every device to escape, his heart grew low and faint within him, giving up the conflict; he felt a dull buzzing in his ears, and a dull throbbing in his breast.

But thinking was not so easy a matter as it seemed. Think it over? How was he to think it over? If it were possible to imagine the case of a man who, walking serenely over a wide and peaceful country, should suddenly, with the softest, scarcely audible, roll of the pebbles under his feet, see the earth yawn before him and find himself on the brink of a fearful precipice, that would have been like his case: but not so bad as his case, for the man would have it in his power to draw back, to retire to the peaceful fields behind: whereas, to Mr. Sandford, there were no peaceful fields, but a gulf all round that one spot of undermined earth on which he stood. Presently he found himself at his own door, very tired and a little dazed in mind, thinking of that precipice, of nothing more distinct. The house stood very solid, very tranquil, its red roof all illumined with the last level line of the sun, the garden stretching into shady corners under the trees, the flower-beds blazing in lavish colours, the little lawn all burnt bare by the ardent sun and worn with the feet of the tennis players: all so peaceful, certain, secure—an old-established home with deep foundations, and the assured, immovable look of household tranquillity and peace. If the walls had been tottering, the garden relapsing into weeds and wildness, he would not have been surprised—that would have been suitable to his circumstances. The thing unsuitable was to come back to that trim order and well-being, to that modest wealth and comfort and beauty, and to know that all this too, like himself, was on the edge of the precipice. Tired as he was, he went round the garden before he went in, and gazed wistfully at the pleasant dwelling with its open windows, wondering, when the next shock of the earthquake came, whether it would all fall to pieces like a house of cards, and everybody become aware that the earth was rent and a great chasm yawning before the peaceful door.

He never seemed to have realised, before now, how full of modest luxury and exquisite comfort that house was. It was not yet covered up and dismantled, though the fingers of the maid-servants had been itching to get at that delightful task since ever "the family" left. All was empty and still, but all in good order; no false pretension or show, everything temperate and well chosen; rich, soft carpets in which the foot sank, curtains hanging in graceful folds, the cosiest chairs, Italian cabinets, Venice glass, pictures, not only of his own but of many contemporary artists—a delightful interior, without a bare corner or vacant spot anywhere. He went over it with a sort of despairing pleasure and admiration, his head aching and giddy, with a sense that at any moment the next shock might come, and everything collapse like the shadows of a dream. Presently he was served with his dinner, which he could not eat, in the cool dining-room, with a large window opening to the garden and the sweet air breathing about him as he sat down at the vacant table. What a mockery of all certitude and safety it was!—for nothing could seem more firmly established, more solid and secure. If he had been a prince of the blood he might have had a more splendid dwelling, but not more comfort, more pleasantness. All that a sober mind could desire was there—the utmost refinement of comfort, beautiful things all around, every colour subdued into perfection, no noise or anything to break the spell. He was glad that the others were absent—it was the only alleviation to the dismay within him. There would have been questions as to what was the matter—"Are you ill, Edward?" "What is wrong with papa?" and other such questions, which he could not have borne.

Afterwards he went into the studio. The first thing that caught his eye was the glow of that piece of drapery which he had painted under the keen stimulant of the first warning. It had been a stimulant then, and he was startled by the splendour of the colour he had put into that piece of stuff—the roundness of it, the clear transparence of the shadows. It stood out upon the picture like something by another hand, painted in another age. Had he done that only a few hours ago—he with the same brushes which had produced the rest of the picture which looked so pale and insignificant beside it? How had he done it? it made all the rest of the picture fade. He recognised in a moment the jogtrot, the ordinary course of life, and against it the flush of the sudden inspiration, the stronger handling, the glory and glow of the colour. He had never done anything better in his life; he whose pictures were drugs in the market, who had not a commission to look forward to. He stood and looked at it for a long time, growing sadder and sadder. He was not a man who had failed, and who could rail against the world; he was a man who had succeeded; not a painter in England but would laugh out if any one said that Sandford had been a failure. Why, who had been successful if he had not? they would have said. He had not a word to say against fate. Nobody was to blame, not even himself, seeing that now, in the midst of all, he could still paint like that. He knew the value of that as well as any man could know it. He could not shut his eyes to it because he himself had done it. If he saw such a bit of painting in a young fellow's picture he would say, "Well done;" he would say, "Paint like that, and you have your fortune in your own hand." Ah, but he was himself no longer a young fellow. Success was not before him; he had grasped her, held her, and now it seemed his day was past.

It is never cheerful to have to allow that your day is past. But there are circumstances which make it less difficult. Sometimes a man accepts gracefully enough that message of dismissal. Then he will retire with a certain dignity, enjoying the ease which he has purchased with his hard work, and looking on henceforward at the struggle of the others, not sorry, perhaps, or at least saying to the world that he is not sorry, to be out of that conflict. Mr. Sandford said to himself that in other circumstances he might have been capable of this; might have laid aside his pencil, occupied himself with guiding the younger, helping the less strong, standing umpire, perhaps, in the strife, giving place to those who represented the future, and whose day was but beginning. Such a retirement must always seem a fit and seemly thing: but not now; not in what he felt was but the fulness of his career; not, above all—and this gave the sting to all—not while he was still depending upon his profession for his daily bread. His daily bread, and what was worse than that, the daily bread of those he loved. How many things that simple phrase involved! Oh for the simplicity of those days when it meant but what it said! He asked himself with a curious, fantastic, half-amused, half-despairing curiosity whether it had ever meant mere bread? Bread and a little fruit, perhaps; a cake, and a draught from a spring in the primitive Eastern days when the phrase was invented. "Day by day our daily bread:" a loaf like that of Elijah which the angel brought him: the cakes of manna in the wilderness of which only enough was gathered to suffice for one day: and the tent at night to retire to, or a cave, perhaps—a shelter which cost nothing. How different now was daily bread; so many things involved in it, that careful product of many men's work, the house which was his home: and all the costly nameless necessities, so much more than food and clothing; the dainty and pleasant things, the flowers and gardens, the amusements, the trifles that make life delightful and sweet. Give us our daily bread: had it ever been supposed to mean all that? All these many years these necessities had been supplied, and all had gone on as if it were part of the constitution of the world. But now the time had come when the machinery was stopped, when everything was brought to a conclusion. Mr. Sandford turned his eye from that bit of painting which stood out upon his picture as if the sun had touched it, to the sheaves of old studies and sketches in the portfolios, the half-finished bits about the walls, all those scraps and fragments, full of suggestion, full of beautiful thoughts, which make the studio of a great painter rich. He had thought a few days ago that all this meant wealth. Now his eyes were opened, and he saw that it meant nothing, that all about him was rubbish not worth the collection, and himself, who could work no longer, who was no more good for anything, only one piece of lumber the more, the most valueless of all.

He paused, and tried to say to himself that this was morbid. But it was not morbid, it was true. With that curious hurrying of the thoughts which a great calamity brings about, he had already glimpsed everything, seeing the whole situation and all that was involved. There was a certain sum of money in the bank, no more anywhere, except after his own death. There were his insurances, a little for every one, enough, he had hoped, though in a much changed and subdued manner, to support his wife and the girls, enough for that daily bread of which he had been thinking; but it could not be had till he died; and that was all. There was nothing, nothing more; nothing to live upon, nothing to turn to. If you have losses, if your income is reduced, you can retrench and diminish your expenses. But when everything is cut off in a moment, when you have no income at all? such utter loss paralyses the unfortunate. He stood in his studio with a sort of vague smile upon his face, and something of the imbecility of utter helplessness taking possession of him. Everything cut off. Nothing to turn to. Vague visions passed through his mind of the expenses of that seaside house, for instance, which could not be got rid of now; of Lizzie's fifty pounds a year which he had promised not without forebodings; of Jack's fee of two guineas which the children had all made so merry about; of the easy course of their existence, their life, which was so blameless, so innocent, so kind: they were all ready to give, ready to be hospitable; none of the family could see another in want and not eagerly offer what they had. Good God! and to think they had nothing, nothing! It was not a question of enough, it was that there was nothing; that all the streams were closed, and all the doors shut, and the successful man, with his large income, had suddenly become like a navvy out of work, like a dock labourer, or whatever was most pitifully unprovided for in the world.

It made Mr. Sandford's brain whirl. So much in the bank, and after that nothing; and all the liberal life going on; the servants, who could not be sent off at a moment's notice; the house, which could not be abandoned; the family, all so cheerful in their false security, who had no presentiment of evil. He asked himself what people did who were ruined? He had no great acquaintance with such things. What did they do? He was very helpless. He could not realise the possibility of breaking up the house, having no home; of dispersing all the pleasant things which had been part of his being so long; of stopping short— — He could not understand how such things were done. And those people who were ruined generally had something upon which they could fall back. A merchant could begin again. He might have friends who would help him to a new start, and there was always hope that he might do as well at last as at first. But an artist (at sixty) could have no new start. The public would have none of him. He had done his best; he could not begin anew. His career when once closed was over, and nothing more could be made of it. He remembered with a forlorn self-reproach of having himself said that So-and-so should retire; that it would be more dignified to give up work before work gave him up. Ah! so easy a thing to say, so cruel a thing to say; but he had not realised that it was cruel, or that such an end was cruel. He had never supposed it possible that such a thing could happen to himself.

The insurances: yes, there were always the insurances: a thousand pounds for each child, that was the calculation they had made. They had said to each other in the old times, Mary and he, that they never could save money enough to make any appreciable provision for so many children, but that if they could but secure for each a thousand pounds, that would always be something. It would help to give the boys a start; it would be something for the girls. That the boys should all have professions in which they would be doing well, and the girls husbands to provide for them, had seemed too commonplace a certainty even to be dwelt upon: and a thousand pounds is never to be despised; it would help the young ones over any early struggle, it would make all the difference. "So long as we live," Mrs. Sandford had said, "they will always have us to fall back upon: and afterwards—what a thing it would have been for us, Edward, to have a thousand pounds to the good to begin upon!" They had thought they made everything safe so, for the young ones. Mr. Sandford, indeed, still felt a faint lightening of his heart as he thought of the insurances. It had always done him good to think of them; that would be something at least to leave behind. But then it was necessary first that he should die.

He had never thought urgently of that necessity. So long as there is nothing pressing about it, no appearance of its approach, it is easy enough to speak of that conclusion. Sometimes there is even a pensive pleasure in it. "When I am out of the way," "When our day is over," are things quite simple to say. For of course that must come one time or another, as everybody knows. It is more serious, but still not anything very bad, to speak now and then of what is to be done "if anything happens." These things make but little impression upon the mind, even when old age is on its way. And Mr. Sandford at sixty had as yet felt very few premonitions of old age. He had called himself an old man with a laugh, for his eye was not dim, nor his natural force abated; and it was still pleasantly absurd to think that he could be supposed an old man. But now all this took a different aspect. He felt no older, indeed, but his position was altogether changed. In the shock of his new circumstances he stood helpless, not knowing how to meet this unfeared, unthought-of contingency. But his mind went off with a spring to further eventualities. The only comfort was this, they had a thousand pounds apiece laid up for them. But it would be necessary first that he should die.

Thinking it all over, he thought, on the whole, that this was the best thing that could happen. The changes which he surveyed with such a sense of impossibility, not knowing how they could be brought about, would become quite natural if he died. There was always a change on the death of the father. It was the natural time for remodelling life, for altering everything. The family would not be able, of course, to remain in this house, to keep up their present superstructure of existence: but then in the change of circumstances that would seem quite natural and they would not feel it. They could put everything, then, upon a simpler footing. And they would have an income, not much of an income, perhaps, but yet something that would come in punctually to the day, and which would be independent of anything they did, which would have nothing to do with picture dealers or patrons of art, or the changes of taste that affected them. What a thing that was, when one came to think of it, to have an income—something which came in all the same whether you worked or not, whether you were ill or well, whether you were in a good vein and could get on with your picture, or whether it dragged and did not satisfy you! It gave him a sensation of pleasure to think of it: but then he reflected on the one preliminary which was not so easy to bring about, which no planning of his could accomplish just when it was wanted, just when it would be of most use.

For before this state of things could ensue, it would be necessary that Mr. Sandford should be dead; and so far as he was aware there was no immediate prospect of anything of the kind. People do not die when it is most necessary, when it would be most expedient. It is a thing independent of your own will, horribly uncertain, happening just when it is not wanted. This difficulty, when he had begun to take a little comfort in the possible arrangement of everything, sent the painter back into all the confusion of miserable thoughts. Was it possible that he was in circumstances which made it impossible for him to do anything, even to die?

CHAPTER V

Mr. Sandford went down next day to the seaside to join his family. They had got a very pleasant house, in full sight of the sea. "What was the use of going to the sea at all," Mrs. Sandford said, "unless you got the full good of it? All the sunsets and effects, and its aspect at every hour of the day, which was so very different from having merely glimpses of it—that is what my husband likes," she said. And of course this meant the most expensive place. He was met at the station by his wife and little Mary, the youngest, who was always considered papa's favourite. The others had all gone along the coast with a large pic-nic party, some of them in a boat, some riding—for there were fine sands—and a delightful gallop along that crisp firm road, almost within the flash of the waves, was most invigorating. "They all look ever so much the better for it already," said the fond mother.

"There was not much the matter with them before that I could see."

"Oh, nothing the matter! But they do so enjoy the sea. And I find there are a great many people here whom we know—more than usual; and a great deal going on."

"There is generally a good deal going on."

"My dear Edward, staying behind has not been good for you; you are looking pale; and I never heard you grudge the children their little pleasures before."

"I stayed at home, papa," said little Mary, not willing to be unappreciated, "to be the first to see you."

"You are always a good little girl," said the father gratefully.

"I assure you they were all anxious to stay: but I did not think you would like them to give up a pleasure," said Mrs. Sandford, never willing to have any of her children subjected to an unfavourable comparison.

"No; oh no," he said, with a sigh. It was almost impossible not to feel a grudge at the thought of that careless enjoyment, no one taking any thought; but he could not burst out with any disclosures of his trouble before little Mary, looking up wistfully in his face with a child's sensitiveness to the perception of something wrong. Mary was more ready to perceive this than Mrs. Sandford, who only thought that her husband was perhaps a little out of temper, or annoyed by some trifling matter, or merely affected by the natural misanthropy of three days' solitude. She clasped his arm caressingly with her hand as she led him along.

"You have got some cobwebs into your mind," she said, "but the sea breezes will soon blow them away."

The sea breezes were very fresh; the sea itself spread out under the sunshine a dazzling stretch of blue; the wide vault of heaven all belted with lines of summer cloud, "which landward stretched along the deep" like celestial countries far away. The air was filled with the soft plash of the water, the softened sound of voices. The whole population seemed out of doors, and all in full enjoyment of the heavenly afternoon and the sights and sounds of the sea. Walking along through these holiday groups, with his wife by his side and his little girl holding his hand, Mr. Sandford felt an unreasonable calm—a sense of soothing quiet—come over him. He could not dismiss the phantom which overshadowed him, but he felt for the moment that he could ignore it. It was necessary that he should ignore it. He could not communicate to his wife so tragical a discovery there and then, in her ease and cheerful holiday mood. He must prepare her for it. Not all in a moment could that revelation burst upon her. Poor Mary! so happy in her children, so full of their plans and pleasures, so secure in the certainty of prosperous life: even the child, strange to think it, understood him better, being nearer, he supposed, to those springs of life where there are no shades of intervening feeling, but all is either happiness or despair. A profound sorrow for these innocent creatures came into his mind; he could not overcloud them, either the mother or the child. They were so glad to have him again; so proud to walk on either side of him, pointing out everything: and all was so happy, were it not for one thing; nothing to trouble them, all well, all full of pleasure, confidence, health, lightheartedness; not a cloud—except that one.

"You have been tiring yourself—doing too much while you have been alone; the servants have made you uncomfortable; they have been pulling everything, to pieces, though I left the most stringent orders—"

"No, the servants were very good; they disturbed nothing, though they were longing to get at it."

"They always are; they take a positive pleasure in making the house look as desolate as possible—as if nobody was ever going to live in it any more."

"Nobody going to live in it more!" he repeated the words with a faint smile. "No—on the contrary, it looked the most liveable place I ever saw. I never felt its home-look so much."

"It is a nice little place," she said, with a little pressure of his arm. "Whatever may happen to the children in after life, we can always feel that they have had a happy youth and a bright home."

"What should happen to them?" he said, alarmed with a sudden fear that she must know.

"Oh, nothing, I hope, but what is good; but the first change in the family always makes one think. I hope you won't mind, Edward: Lance Moulton is here."

"Oh, he is here!"

"If it is really to be so, Edward, don't you think it is better they should see as much of each other as possible?" his wife said, with another tender pressure of his arm. "And somehow, when there is a thing of that kind in the air, everything seems quickened; I am sure I can't tell how it is. It gives a 'go' to all they are doing. There are no end of plans and schemes among them. Of course, Lance has a friend or two about, and the Dropmores are here, who are such friends of our girls."

"And all is fun and nonsense, I suppose?"

"Well, if you call it so—all pleasure, and kindness, and real delightful holiday. Oh, Edward," said Mrs. Sandford, with the ghost of a tear in her eye, "don't let us check it! It is the brightest time of their lives."

The sunset was blazing in glory upon the sea, the belts of cloud all reddening and glowing, soft puffs of vapour like roses floating across the blue of the sky. And the air full of young voices softened and musical, children playing, lovers wandering about, happy mothers watching the sport, all tender gaiety, and security, and peace. Everything joyful—save one thing. "No; God forbid that I should check it," he said hastily, with a sigh that might have been a groan.

They all came back not long after, full of high spirits and endless talk; they were all glad to see their father, who had never been any restraint upon their pleasure, whose grave, gentle presence had never checked or stilled them. They were sure of his sympathy more or less. If he did not share their fun, he had at least never discouraged it. And soon in the plenitude of their own affairs they forgot him, as was so natural, and filled the room with laughing consultations over to-morrow's pleasure, and plans for it. "What are we going to do?" they all cried, one after another, even Lizzie and Lance, coming in a little dazzled from the balcony, where they had been enjoying the last fading lights of the ending day, while the others had clamoured for lamps and candles inside; "What are we going to do?" Mrs. Sandford sat beaming upon them, hearing all the suggestions, offering a new idea now and then. "I must know to-night, that the hampers may be got ready," she said; and then there was an echoing laugh all round. "Mother's always so practical." Mr. Sandford sat a little outside of that lively circle with a book in his hand. But he was not reading; he was watching them with a strange fascination; not willing to check them; oh no! feeling a helpless sort of wonder that they should play such pranks on the edge of the precipice, and that none of them should divine—that even his wife should not divine! The animated group, full in the light of the lamps—girls and young men in the frank familiarity of the family interrupting each other, contradicting each other, discussing and arguing—was as charming a study as a painter could have desired; the mother in the midst with her pencil in her hand and a sheet of white paper on the table before her, which threw back the light; and behind, the lovers stealing in out of the soft twilight shadows, the faint glimmer of distant sea and sky. He watched it with a strange dull ache under the pleasure of the father and the painter: the light touching those graceful outlines, shining in those young eyes, the glimmer of shining hair, the play of animated features, the soft, dreamlike, suggestive shadows of the two behind. And yet the precipice yawning, gaping at their feet, though nobody knew.

"Papa," said suddenly a small voice in his ear, "I am not going to-morrow. I want to stay with you."

"My little Mary! But I am a dull old fellow, not worth staying with."

"You are sorry about something, papa!"

"Sorry? There are a great many things in the world to be sorry about," he said, stroking her brown head. The child had clasped her hands about his arm, and was nestling close up to him whispering. They were altogether outside of the lively group at the table. This little consoler comforted Mr. Sandford more than words could say.

It was thus that the holiday life went on. The young people were always consulting what to do, making up endless excursions and expeditions, Mrs. Sandford always explaining for them. What was the use of being at the seaside if they did not take full advantage of it? What was the use of coming to a new part of the country if they did not see everything? Sometimes she went with them, compelled by the addition of various strangers with whom the girls could not go without a chaperon; sometimes stayed at home with her husband, calculating where they would be by this time; whether they had found a pleasant spot for their luncheon; when they might be expected back. Meanwhile, Mr. Sandford took long solitary walks—very long, very solitary—along the endless line of the sands, within sight and sound of the sea. Little Mary and her next brother, the schoolboy, always started with him; but the fascination of the rocks and pools was too much for these little people, and the father, not ill-pleased, went on with a promise of picking them up again on his way back. He would walk on and on for the whole of the fresh shining morning, with the sea on one side and the green country on the other, and all the wonderful magical lights of the sky and water shining as if for him alone. They beguiled him out of himself with their miraculous play and shimmer and wealth of heavenly reflection; and sometimes he seemed to feel a higher sensation still—the feeling as of a silent great Companion who filled the heavenly space, yet moved with him, an all-embracing, all-responsive sympathy, till he thought of God coming down to the cool of the garden and walking with His creatures, and all his trouble seemed to breathe away in a heavenly hush, which every little wave repeated, softly lapping at his feet.

But when he came back into the midst of his cheerful family other subjects got the upper hand. There was not the least harm in the gaiety that was about him—not the least harm; it was mere exuberance of youthful life and pleasure. If things had been running their usual course, and his usual year's work had been in front of him, Mr. Sandford said to himself that he too would have come out to the door to see the children start on their expeditions, as his wife did, with pleasure in their good looks, and in the family union and happiness. He might have grumbled a little over Harry's idleness, or even shaken his head over the expense; but he too would have liked it—he would have admired his young ones, and taken pleasure in seeing them happy. But to stand by and watch all that, and know that presently the revenue which kept it all up would stop, and the ground be cut from under their feet, sheer down, like a precipice! Already he had begun to familiarise himself with this idea. It had a sort of paralysing effect, as well as one of panic and horror. It is not a thing that happens often. People grow poorer, or even they get ruined at a blow, but there is generally something remaining upon which economy will tell; he went over these differences in his lonely hours, imagining a hundred cases. A merchant, for instance, who ruins himself by speculation, if he is an honourable man, has means at his disposal of trying again, or at least can get a situation in an office (at the worst), where he will still have an income—a steady income, though it may be small; his friends, and the people who had business relations with him, would be sure to exert themselves to secure him that; or if his losses were but partial, of course nothing could be easier than to retrench and live at a lower rate. So Mr. Sandford said to himself. But what can a few economies do when at a critical moment, at a period close at hand, all incoming must cease, and nothing remain? It did not now give him the violent shock of sensation which he had felt at first when this fact came uppermost. He had become accustomed to it. It was not après moi, but in three months or so, the deluge: an end to everything, no half measures, no retrenchment, but the end. He began to wonder when that time came what would be done. The house could be sold, and all that was in it, but where then would they go for shelter? They would have to pay for the poorest lodgings, and at least there was nothing to pay for the house. Mr. Sandford was not a man of business, he was a man of few resources; he did not know what to do, or where to turn when his natural occupation failed him.

These thoughts went through his mind in a painful round. Three months or so, and then an end of everything. Three months, and then the precipice so near that the next step must be over it. Perhaps in other circumstances, or if he had not been known to be so near the head of his profession, he might have thought of artists' work of some other kind which he could do. He might have tried to illustrate books, to take up one of the art manufactures; might have become a designer, a decorator, something that would bring in money. But in this respect he was so helpless, he knew no more what to do than the most ignorant; his heart failed him when he tried to penetrate into the darkness of that future. The only thing that came uppermost was the thought of the insurances, and of the thousand pounds for each which the children would have. It was not very much, but still it was something, a something real and tangible, not like a workman's wages for work, which may fail in a moment as soon as he fails to please his employer, or loses his skill, or grows too old for it. It had never occurred to Mr. Sandford before how precarious these wages are, how little to be relied on. To think of a number of people depending for their whole living upon the skill of one man's hand, upon the clearness of his sight, the truth of his instincts, even the fashion of the moment! It seems, when you look at it in the light of a discovery such as that which he had made, so mad, so fatal! A thing that may cease in a moment as if it had never been, yet with all the complicated machinery of life built upon it, based on the strange theory that it would go on for ever! On the other hand a thousand pounds is a solid thing; it would be a certainty for each of them. Harry might go to one of the colonies and get an excellent start with a thousand pounds in his pocket. Jack would no doubt be startled into energy by the sense of having something which it would be fatal to lose, yet which could not be lived upon. A thousand pounds would make all the difference to Lizzie on her marriage. When he thought of his wife a quiver of pain went over him, and yet he tried to calculate all the chances there would be for her. All friends would be stirred in sympathy for her; they would get her a pension, they would gather round her: it would be made easy for her to break up this expensive way of living, and begin on a smaller footing. There would be the house, which would bring her in a little secure income if it was let. Whatever she had would be secure—it would be based on something solid, certain—not on a man's work, which might lose its excellence or go out of fashion. He felt himself smile with a kind of pleasure at the contemplation of this steady certainty—which he never had possessed, which he never could possess, but which poor Mary, with a pension and the rent of the house, would at last obtain. Poor Mary! his lip quivered when he thought of her. He wondered if the children would absorb her interest as much when he was no longer in the background, whether she would be able to find in them all that she wanted, and consolation for his absence. It was not with any sense of blame that this thought went through his mind. Blame her! oh no. To think of her children was surely a mother's first duty. She was not aware that her husband wanted consolation and help more than they did. How could she know when he did not tell her? And he felt incapable of telling her. He had meant to do it. When he came he had intended as soon as possible to prepare her for it, to lead by degrees to that revelation which could not but be given. But to break in upon all their innocent gaieties, to stop her as she stood kissing her hand to the merry cavalcade as they set out, her eyes shining with a mother's delight and pride; to call her away from among her pretty daughters (she, her husband thought the fairest of them all), and their pleasant babble about pleasures past and to come, and pour black despair into the cheerful heart, how could he do it, how could any one do it? Such happiness was sacred. He could not interrupt it, he could not destroy it; it was pathetic, tragic, beyond words: on the edge of the precipice! Oh no, no! not now, he could not tell her. Let the holidays be over, let common life resume again, and then—unless by the grace of God something else might happen before.

They all noticed, however, that papa was dull—which was the way in which it struck the young people—that he had no sympathy with their gaiety, that he was "grumpy," which was what it came to. Lizzie thought that this probably arose from dissatisfaction with her marriage, and was indignant. "If he doesn't think Lance good enough, I wonder what would please him. Did he expect one of the princes to propose to me?" she cried.

"Oh, Lizzie, my love, don't speak so of your father!"

"Well, mamma, he should not look at us so," cried the girl.

Mrs. Sandford herself was a little indignant too. Her sympathies were all with the children. She saw disapproval in his subdued looks, and was ready at any moment to spring to arms in defence of her children. And indeed sometimes, in his great trouble, which no one divined, Mr. Sandford would sometimes become impatient.

"I wish," he would say, "that Jack would do something—does he never do anything at all? It frets me to see a young man so idle."

"My dear Edward!" cried his wife, "it is the Long Vacation. What should he have to do?"

"And Harry?" Mr. Sandford said.

"Poor boy! You know he would give his little finger to have anything to do. He has nothing to do. How can he help that? When we go back to town you must really put your shoulder to the wheel. Among all your friends surely, surely, something could be got for Harry," said his mother, thus turning the tables. "And in the meantime," she added, "to get all the health he can, and the full good of the sea, is certainly the best thing the poor fellow could do."

What answer could be made to this? Mr. Sandford went out for his walk—that long silent walk, in which the great Consoler came down from amid all the silvery lights and shining skies, and walked with him in the freshness of the morning, all silent in tenderness and great solemnity and awe.

CHAPTER VI

"Unless, by the grace of God, something should happen"—that was what he kept saying to himself when he reflected on the disclosure which must be made when the seaside season was over. The great events of life rarely happen according to our will. A man cannot die when he wishes it, though there should be every argument in favour of such an event, and its advantages most palpable. The moment passes in which that conclusion would have all the force and satisfactory character of a great tragedy, and a dreary postscript of existence drivels on, destructive of all dignity and appropriateness. We live when we should do much better to die, and we die sometimes when every circumstance calls upon us to live.

Most people will think that it was a very dreary hope that moved Mr. Sandford's mind—perhaps even that it was not the expedient of a brave man to desire to leave his wife and children to endure the change and the struggle from which he shrank in his own person. But this was not how it appeared to him. He thought, and with some reason, that the change which becomes inevitable on the death of the head of a house is without humiliation, without the pang of downfall which would be involved in an entire reversal of life which had not that excuse; he thought that everybody who knew him would regret the change, and that every effort would be made to help those who were left behind. It would be no shame to them to accept that help; it would seem to them a tribute to his position rather than pity for them. His wife would believe that her husband, a great painter, one of the first of the day, had fully earned that recognition, and would be proud of the pension or the money raised for her as of a monument in his honour. And then the insurances. There could be no doubt, he said to himself, with a rueful smile, that so much substantial money would be much better to have than a man who could earn nothing, who had become incapable, whose work nobody wanted. He had no doubt whatever that it would be by far the best solution. It would rouse the boys by a sharp and unmistakable necessity; it might, he thought, be the making of the boys, who had no fault in particular except the disposition to take things easily, which was the weakness of this generation. And as for the others, they would be taken care of—no doubt they would be taken care of. Their condition would appeal to the kindness of every friend who had ever bought a "Sandford" or thought it an honour to know the painter. He would even himself be restored to honour and estimation by the act of dying, which often is a very ingratiating thing, and makes the public change its opinion. All these arguments were so strongly in favour of it that to think there was no means of securing it depressed Mr. Sandford's mind more than all. By the grace of God. But it is certain that the Disposer of events does not always see matters as His creatures see them. No one can make sure, however warmly such a decree might be wished for, or even prayed for, that it will be given. If only that would happen! But it was still more impossible to secure its happening than to open a new market for the pictures, or cause commissions to pour in again.

It may be asked whether Mr. Sandford's conviction, which was so strong on this subject, ever moved him to do anything to bring about his desire. It was impossible, perhaps, that the idea should not have crossed his mind—

"When we ourselves can our demission make With a bare bodkin."

And we can scarcely say that it was, like Hamlet, the fear of something after death that restrained him. It was a stronger sentiment still. It was the feeling that to give one's self one's dismissal is quite a different thing. It is a flight—it is a running away; all the arguments against the selfishness of desiring to leave his wife and children to a struggle from which he had escaped came into action against that. What would be well if accomplished by the grace of God would be miserable if done by the will of the man who might be mistaken in his estimate of the good it would do. And then another practical thought, more tragical than any in its extreme materialism and matter-of-fact character, it would vitiate the insurances! If the children were to gain nothing by his death, then it would certainly be better for them that he should live. On that score there could be no doubt. This made suicide as completely out of the question from a physical point of view as it was already from a spiritual. He could not discharge himself from God's service on earth, though he should be very thankful if God would discharge him; and he could not do anything to endanger the precious provision he had made for his family. It can scarcely be said that Mr. Sandford considered this case at leisure or with comparison of the arguments for and against, for his decision was instinctive and immediate; nevertheless the idea floated uppermost sometimes in the surging and whirl up and down of many thoughts, but always to be dismissed in the same way.

Two or three weeks had passed in this way when one evening Mr. Sandford received a letter from Daniells, the dealer, inviting him to join a party on the Yorkshire moors. Daniells was well enough off to be able to deny himself nothing. He was not a gentleman, yet the sports that gentlemen love were within reach of his wealth, and gentlemen not so well off as he showed much willingness to share in his good things. Some fine people whose names it was a pleasure to read were on his list, and some painters who were celebrated enough to eclipse the fine people. That all these should be gathered together by a man who was as ignorant as a pig, and not much better bred, was wonderful; but so it was. Perhaps the fact that Daniells was really at heart a good fellow had something to do with it: but even had this not been the case, it is probable that he could still have found guests to shoot on his moor, and eat the birds they had shot. Mr. Sandford was no sportsman, and at first he had little inclination to accept. It was his wife who urged him to do so.

"You are not enjoying Broadbeach as you usually do," she said; "you are bored by it. Oh, don't tell me, Edward, I can see it in your eyes."

"If you think so, my dear, no denial of mine—"

"No," she said, shaking her head; "nothing you say will change my opinion. I am dreadfully sorry, for I am fond of the place; but I have made up my mind already never to come here again: for you are bored—it is as plain as possible: you want a change: you must go."

"It is not much of a change to visit Daniells," said Mr. Sandford.

"Oh, it isn't Daniells; it's the company, and the distance, and all you will find there. I have no objection to Mr. Daniells, Edward."

"Nor I; he is a good fellow in spite of his 'h's.'"

"I don't care about his 'h's.' He's very hospitable and very friendly, and all the nice people go to him. I saw in the papers that Lord Okeham was there. You might be able to speak a word for Harry."

Mr. Sandford smiled. "I am to go, then, as a business speculation," he said; but his smile faded away very soon, for he reflected that Lord Okeham was the first to give him that sensation of being wanted no longer, of having nobody to employ him, which had risen to such a tragic height since then.

"Don't laugh," said his wife. "I do think indeed it is your duty—anything that may help on the children; and you do like Mr. Daniells, Edward."

"Yes, I do like Daniells; he is a very good fellow."

"And the change will do you good. You must go."

It was arranged so almost without any voluntary action on his part. His wife's anxiety that he should "speak a word for Harry" seemed to him half-pathetic, half-ridiculous in what he knew to be the position of affairs; but then she did not know. It can scarcely be said that it was other than a relief to him to leave his family to their own light-hearted devices, or that the young ones were not at least half-pleased when he went away. "Papa was not a bit like himself," they said; probably it was because the heat was too much for him (he preferred cold weather), and the freshness of the moors would put him all right. Mrs. Sandford was by no means willing to confess to herself that she, too, was relieved by her husband's departure. It was the first time she had ever been conscious of that feeling in thirty years of married life; but she, too, said that he would be the better of the freshness of the moors, and they all gave themselves up to "fun" with a new rush of pleasure when his grave countenance was away.

"I am sure he did not mean it," said Lizzie, "but I could not help feeling that it was poor Lance that was the cause."

"Nothing of the sort, my dear," said Mrs. Sandford. "Your father would have told you if he had any objections. No; I know what it is; he is very anxious about the boys—and so am I."

No one, however, who had seen her among them could have believed that Mrs. Sandford was very anxious. She was so glad that they should enjoy themselves. Afterwards, when the holidays were over, when they were all back in town again, then something, no doubt, must be done about Harry. He was very thoughtless, to be sure; he took no trouble about what was going to happen to him. Mrs. Sandford threw off any shade of distress, however, by saying to herself that now his father was fully roused to the necessity of doing something, now that he was about to meet Lord Okeham and other influential people, something must be found for Harry, and then all would go well. But the look in her husband's eyes haunted her, nevertheless, for the rest of the day. She had gone to the railway with him to see him off, as she always did, and when the train was just moving, he looked at her, waving his hand to her. The look in his eyes was so strange and so sad, that Mrs. Sandford felt disposed to rush after her husband by the next train. Failing that, she drew her veil over her face as she turned away and shed tears, she could not tell why, as if he had been going away never to return. How ridiculous! how absurd! when he was only a little out of sorts and sure to be set right by the freshness of the moors. The impression very soon wore out, and the young people had already organised a little impromptu dance for the evening, which gave Mrs. Sandford plenty to do.

"It looks a little like taking advantage of your father's absence—as if you were glad he was gone."

"Not at all," they all cried. "What a dreadful idea! The only thing is that it would have bored him horribly; otherwise," added Harry, "we are always glad of my father's company," with an air of protection and patronage which made the others laugh. And Mrs. Sandford keenly enjoyed the dance, and felt it better that her husband's face, never so grave before, should not be there to over-shadow the evening's entertainment. He would be so much more in his element discussing light and shade with the other R.A.s, or talking a little moderate politics with Lord Okeham, or breathing in the freshness of the moors.

And he did like the freshness of the moors, and the talk of his brother artists, and the discussions among the men. It was entirely a man's party, and perhaps a very domestic man like Mr. Sandford, a little neglected amid the exuberances of a young family, his very wife drawn away from him by the exigencies of their amusements, is specially open to the occasional refreshment of a party of his fellows, when congenial pursuits and matured views, and something of a like experience—at all events something which is a real experience of life—draw individuals together. The "sport" of the painters was apt to be interrupted by realisations of the "effects" about them, and by discussions on various artistic-scientific points which only masters in the art could settle; and that semi-professional flavour of the party was extremely interesting to the other men, the public personages and society magnates, who found it very piquant to be thrown amid the painters, and who were inspired thereby to talk their best, and tell their most entertaining stories. No atmosphere of failure accompanied Mr. Sandford into this circle, which was kept hilarious by the host's jovialities and social mistakes. If anybody knew that Daniells kept in his inner room three "Sandfords" which he could not sell, there was no hint of that knowledge in anything that was said, or in the manner of the other painters towards their fellow, to whom all appealed as to as great an authority as could be found on all questions of art. He was restored, thus, to the position which, indeed, nobody could take from him, though he should never sell a picture again. It soothed him to feel and see that, to all his brethren, he was as much as ever one of the first painters of his time, and to give his opinion and sustain it with the experience of his long professional life, and much experiment in art. A forlorn hope had been in his mind that Daniells might have some good news for him; that he might say some day, "That was all a false alarm, old man—I've sold the pictures;" but this unfortunately did not come to pass. Daniells never said it was a false alarm; he even said some things in his rough but not unkindly way which to Mr. Sandford's ear, quickened by trouble, confirmed the disaster; but perhaps Daniells, who had no particular delicacy of perception, did not intend this.

The change, however, did Mr. Sandford a great deal of good: though sometimes, when he found himself alone, the settled shadow of calamity which had closed upon his life, and which must soon be known to all, came over him with almost greater force than at first. It was but seldom that he was alone, when he was indoors: yet now and then he would find himself on the moors in the sun-setting, when the western sky was still one blaze of yellow or orange light, varied by bands of cloudy red, with the low hills and sweeps of moor standing black against that waning brightness which, magnificent as it was, sent out little light. Mr. Sandford did not compare his own going out of practical life and possibility, yet preservation of a glow of fame which neither warmed nor enlightened, with that show in the west. People seldom see allegories of their own disaster. But as he strayed along with the sense of dreariness in his heart which the dead and spectral aspect of hill and tree was so well calculated to give, his own circumstances came back to him in tragic glimpses. He thought of the gay group he had left behind, the heedless young creatures singing and dancing on the edge of the precipice, and of the peaceful home lying silent awaiting them, to which they had no doubt of returning, with all its security of comfort and peace, but on the edge of the precipice too. And he thought of Jack's fee, his two guineas, which they had all taken as the best joke in the world, and of Lizzie, who was to have fifty pounds a year from her father, and of Harry, quite happy and content on his schoolboy allowance; and all this going on as if it were the course of nature, unchangeable as the stars or the pillars of the earth. These things glided before him as he looked over all the inequalities of the moor standing black against the western sky. They were the true facts about him, notwithstanding that in the shelter of this momentary pause he only felt them as at a distance, and less strongly than before realised the ease it would bring if by the grace of God something happened—before—

It was the time of the year when there are various race meetings in the north, and Mr. Daniells had planned to carry his party to the most famous of them. He had his landau and a brake, royally charged with provisions, and filled with his guests. Mr. Sandford had done his best to get off this unnecessary festivity, for which he had little taste. But all his friends, who by this time had begun to perceive that his spirits were not in their usual equable state, resisted and protested. He must come, they said: to leave one behind would spoil the party; he was not to be left alone with all the moorland effects to steal a march upon the other painters. And he had not sufficient energy to stand against their remonstrances. It was easier to yield, and he yielded. The race was not unamusing. Even with all his preoccupation, he took a little pleasure in it, more or less, as most Englishmen do: though it glanced across his mind that somebody might say afterwards, "Sandford was there, amusing himself on the edge of the precipice." These vague voices and glimpses of things were not enough to stand against the remonstrances and banter of his friends: and after all, what did it matter? The plunge over the precipice is not less terrible because you may have performed a dance of despair on the edge. It was about sunset on a lovely September evening when the party set out on their return home. They were merry; not that there had been any excess or indulgence unbecoming of English gentlemen. Daniells, it is true, who was not a gentleman, had, perhaps, a little more champagne under his belt than was good for him. But his guests were only merry, talking a little more loudly than usual about the events of the day and the exploits of the favourite, and settling some moderate bets which neither harmed nor elated any one. Mr. Sandford, who had not betted, was the most silent of party; the lively talk of the others left him free to retire to his own thoughts. He had got rather into a tangle of dim calculations about his insurances, and how the money would be divided, when somebody suddenly called out "Hallo! we've got off the road!"

For some time Mr. Sandford was the only one who paid any attention to this statement. Looking out with a little start, he saw the same scene against which his musings had taken form on previous nights. A sky glowing with a stormy splendour, deep burning orange on the horizon rising through zones of yellow to the daffodil sky above, every object standing out black in the absence of light; not the hedgerows and white line of the road alone, but the blunt inequalities of the moor, here a lump of gorse or gnarled hawthorn bush, there a treacherous hollow with a gleam of water gathered as in a cup. The coachman and grooms had not been so prudent as their masters; their potations had been heavier than champagne. How they had left the road and got upon the moor could never be discovered. It was partly the perplexing glow above and blackness below, partly the fumes of a long day's successive drinkings in their brains; partly, perhaps, as one of the passengers thought, something else. The horses had taken the unusual obstacles on their path with wonderful steadiness at first, but by the time the attention of the gentlemen was fully attracted to what was happening, the coachman had altogether lost control of the kicking and plunging animals. The man was not too far gone to have driven home by the road, but his brain was incapable of any effort to meet such an emergency. He began to flog the horses wildly, to swear at them, to pull savagely at the reins. The groom jumped down to rush to their heads, and in doing so, as they made a plunge at the moment, fell on the roadside, and in a moment more was left behind as the terrified horses dashed on. By this time everybody was roused, and the danger was evident. Mr. Sandford sat quite still; he was not learned about horses, while many of his companions were. One of them got on to the box beside the terrified coachman to try what could be done, the others gave startled and sometimes contradictory suggestions and directions. He was quite calm in the tumult of alarm and eager preparation for any event. He was sensible, profoundly sensible, of the wonderful effect of the scene: the orange glow which no pigments in the world could reproduce, the blackness of the indistinguishable objects which stood up against it like low dark billows of a motionless sea. The shocks of the jolting carriage affected him little, any more than the shouts of the alarmed and excited men. He did not even remark, then, that some sprang off and that others held themselves ready to follow. His sensations were those of perfect calm. He thought of the precipice no more, nor even of the insurances. Some one shook him by the shoulder, but it did not disturb him. The effect was wonderful; the orange growing intense, darker, the yellow light pervading the illuminated sky. And then a sudden wild whirl, a shock of sudden sensation, and he saw or felt no more.

CHAPTER VII

Presently the light came back to Mr. Sandford's eyes. He was lying upon the dry heather on the side of the moor, the brown seed-pods nestling against his cheek, the yellow glow in the west, to which his eyes instinctively turned, having scarcely faded at all since he had looked at it from the carriage. A confused sound of noises, loud speaking, and moans of pain reached him where he lay, but scarcely moved him to curiosity. His first sensation was one of curious ease and security. He did not attempt to budge, but lay quite peacefully smiling at the sunset, like a child. His head was confused, but there was in it a vague sense of danger escaped, and of some kind of puzzled deliverance from he knew not what, which gave the strangest feeling of soothing and rest. He felt no temptation to jump up hastily, to go to the help of the people who were moaning, or to inquire into the accident, as in another case he would have done. He lay still, quite at his ease, hearing these voices as if he heard them not, and smiling with a confused pleasure at the glow of orange light in the sky.

He did not know how long it was till some one knelt down and spoke to him anxiously. "Sandford, are you badly hurt? Sandford, my dear fellow, do you know me? Can you speak to me?"

He burst into a laugh at this address.

"Speak to you? Know you? What nonsense! I am not hurt at all. I am quite comfortable."

"Thank God!" said the other. "Duncan, I fear, has a broken leg, and the coachman is—It was his fault, the unfortunate wretch. Give me your hand, and I'll help you to get up."

To get up? That was quite a different matter. He did not feel the least desire to try. He felt, before trying and without any sense of alarm, that he could not get up; then said to himself that this was nonsense too, and that to lie there, however comfortably, when he might be helping the others, was not to be thought of. He gave his hand accordingly to his friend, and made an effort to rise. But it would have been as easy (he said to himself) for a log of wood to attempt to rise. He felt rather like that, as if his legs had turned to wood—not stone, for that would have been cold and uncomfortable. "I don't know how it is," he said, still smiling, "but I can't budge. There's nothing the matter with me, I'm quite easy and comfortable, but I can't move a limb. I'll be all right in a few minutes. Look after the others. Never mind me." He thought the face of the man who was bending over him looked strangely scared, but nothing more was said. A rug was put over him and one of the cushions of the carriage under his head, and there he lay, vaguely hearing the groans of the man whose leg was broken as (apparently) they moved him, and all the exclamations and questions and directions given by one and another. What was more wonderful was the dying out of that wild orange light in the sky. It paled gradually, as if it had been glowing metal, and the cold night air breathing on it had paled and dwindled that ineffectual fire. A hundred lessening tints and tones of colour—yellows and faint greens, with shades of purple and creamy whiteness breaking the edges—melted and shimmered in the distance. It was like an exhibition got up for him alone, relieved by that black underground, now traversed by gigantic ebony figures of a horse and man, moving irregularly across the moor. A star came out with a keen blue sparkle, like some power of heaven triumphant over that illumination of earth. What a spectacle it was! And all for him alone!

The next thing he was conscious of was two or three figures about him—one the doctor, whose professional touch he soon discovered on his pulse and his limbs. "We are going to lift you. Don't take any trouble; it will give you no pain," some one said. And before he could protest, which he was about to do good-humouredly, that there was no occasion, he found himself softly raised upon some flat and even surface, more comfortable, after all, than the lumps of the heather. Then there was a curious interval of motion along the road, no doubt, though all he saw was the sky with the stars coming gradually out; neither the road nor his bearers, except now and then a dark outline coming within the line of his vision; but always the deep blue of the mid sky shining above. The world seemed to have concentrated in that, and it was not this world, but another world.

He remembered little more, except by snatches; an unknown face—probably the doctor's—looking exceedingly grave, bending over him; then Daniells' usually jovial countenance with all the lines drooping and the colour blanched out of it, and a sound of low voices talking something over, of which he could only make out the words "Telegraph at once;" then, "Too late! It must not be too late. She must come at once." He wondered vaguely who this was, and why there should be such a hurry. And then, all at once, it seemed to him that it was daylight and his wife was standing by his bedside. He had just woke up from what seemed a very long, confused, and feverish night—how long he never knew. But when he woke everything was clear to him. Unless, by the grace of God, something were to happen—Something was about to happen, by the grace of God.

"Mary!" he cried, with a flush of joy. "You here!"

"Of course, my dearest," she said, with a cheerful look, "as soon as I heard there had been an accident."

He took her hand between his and drew her to him. "This was all I wanted," he said. "God is very good; He gives me everything."

"Oh, Edward!" This pitiful protest, remonstrance, appeal to heaven and earth—for all these were in her cry—came from her unawares.

"Yes," he said, "my dear, everything has happened as I desired. I understand it all now. I thought I was not hurt; now I see. I am not hurt, I am killed, like the boy—don't you remember?—in Browning's ballad. Don't be shocked, dear. Why shouldn't I be cheerful? I am not—sorry."

"Oh, Edward!" she cried again, the passion of her trouble exasperated by his composure; "not to leave—us all?"

He held her hand between his, smiling at her. "It was what I wanted," he said—"not to leave you; but don't you believe, my darling, there must be something about that leaving which is not so dreadful, which is made easy to the man who goes away? Certainly, I don't want to leave you; but it's so much for your good—for the children's good—"

"Oh, never, Edward, never!"

"Yes; it's new to you, but I've been thinking about it a long time—so much that I once thought it would almost have been worth the while, but for the insurances, to have—"

"Edward!" She looked at him with an agonised cry.

"No, dear—nothing of the kind. I never would, I never could have done it. It would have been contrary to nature. The accident—was without any will or action of mine. By the grace of God—"

"Edward, Edward! Oh, don't say that; by His hand, heavy, heavy upon us!"

"It is you that should not say that, Mary. If you only knew, my dear. I want you to understand so long as I am here to tell you—"

"He must not talk so much," said the voice of the doctor behind; "his strength must be husbanded. Mrs. Sandford, you must not allow him to exhaust himself."

"Doctor," said Mr. Sandford, "I take it for granted you're a man of sense. What can you do for me? Spin out my life by a few more feeble hours. Which would you rather have yourself? That, or the power of saying everything to the person you love best in the world?"

"Let him talk," said the doctor, turning away; "I have no answer to make. Give him a little of this if he turns faint. And send for me if you want me, Mrs. Sandford."

"Thanks, doctor. That is a man of sense, Mary. I feel quite well, quite able to tell you everything."

"Oh, Edward, when that is the case, things cannot be so bad! If you will only take care, only try to save your strength, to keep up. Oh, my dear! The will to get well does so much! Try! try! Edward, for the love of God."

"My own Mary: always believing that everything's to be done by an effort, as all women do. I am glad it is out of my power. If I were in any pain there might be some hope for you, but I'm in no pain. There's nothing the matter with me but dying. And I have long felt that was the only way."

"Dying?—not when you were with us at the sea?"

"Most of all then," he said, with a smile.

"Oh, Edward, Edward! and I full of amusements, of pleasure, leaving you alone."

"It was better so. I am glad of every hour's respite you have had. And now you'll be able easily to break up the house, which would have been a hard thing and a bitter downfall in my lifetime. It will be quite natural now. They will give you a pension, and there will be the insurance money."

"I cannot bear it," she cried wildly. "I cannot have you speak like this."

"Not when it is the utmost ease to my mind—the utmost comfort—"

She clasped her hands firmly together. "Say anything you wish, Edward."

"Yes, my poor dear." He was very, very sorry for his wife. It burst upon her without preparation, without a word of warning. Oh, he was sorry for her! But for himself it was a supreme consolation to pour it all forth, to tell her everything. "If I were going to be left behind," he said, soothingly, "my heart would be broken: but it is softened somehow to those that are going away. I can't tell you how. It is, though; it is all so vague and soft. I know I'll lose you, Mary, as you lose me, but I don't feel it. My dearest, I had not a commission, not one. And there are three pictures of mine unsold in Daniells' inner shop. He'll tell you if you ask him. The three last. That one of the little Queen and her little Maries, that our little Mary sat for, that you liked so much, you remember? It's standing in Daniells' room; three of them. I think I see them against the wall."

"Edward!"

"Oh no, my head is not going. I only think I see them. And it was the merest chance that the 'Black Prince' sold; and not a commission, not a commission. Think of that, Mary. It is true such a thing has happened before, but I never was sixty before. Do you forget I am an old man, and my day is over?"

"No, no, no," she cried with passion; "it is not so."

"Oh yes; facts are stubborn things—it is so. And what should we have done if our income had stopped in a moment, as it would have done? A precipice before our feet, and nothing, nothing beyond. Now for you, my darling, it will be far easier. You can sell the house and all that is in it. And they will give you a pension, and the children will have something to begin upon."

"Oh, the children!" she cried, taking his hand into hers, bowing down her face upon it. "Oh, Edward, what are the children between you and me?" She cast them away in that supreme moment; the young creatures all so well, so gay, so hopeful. In her despair and passion she flung their crowding images from her—those images which had forced her husband from her heart.

He laughed a low, quiet laugh. "God bless them," he said; "but I like to have you all to myself, you and me only, for the last moment, Mary. You have been always the best wife that ever was—nay, I won't say have been—you are my dear, my wife. We don't understand anything about widows, you and I. Death's nothing, I think. It looks dreadful when you're not going. But God manages all that so well. It is as if it were nothing to me. Mary, where are you?"

"Here, Edward, holding your hand. Oh, my dear, don't you see me?"

"Yes, yes," he said, with a faint laugh, as if ashamed at some mistake he had made, and put his other hand over hers with a slight groping movement. "It's getting late," he said; "it's getting rather dark. What time is it? Seven o'clock? You'll not go down to dinner, Mary? Stay with me. They can bring you something upstairs."

"Go down? Oh, no, no. Do you think I would leave you, Edward?" She had made a little pause of terror before she spoke, for, indeed, it was broad day, the full afternoon sunshine still bright outside, and nothing to suggest the twilight. He sighed again—a soft, pleasurable sigh.

"If you don't mind just sitting by me a little. I see your dear face in glimpses, sometimes as if you had wings and were hovering over me. My head's swimming a little. Don't light the candles. I like the half-light; you know I always did. So long as I can see you by it, Mary. Is that a comfortable chair? Then sit down, my love, and let me keep your hand, and I think I'll get a little sleep."

"It will do you good," said the poor wife.

"Who knows?" he said, with another smile. "But don't let them light the candles."

Light the candles! She could see, where she sat there, the red sunshine falling in a blaze upon a ruddy heathery hill, and beating upon the dark firs which stood out like ink against that background. There is perhaps nothing that so wrings the heart of the watcher as this pathetic mistake of day for night which betrays the eyes from which all light is failing. He lay within the shadow of the curtain, always holding her hand fast, and fell asleep—a sleep which, for a time, was soft and quiet enough, but afterwards got a little disturbed. She sat quite still, not moving, scarcely breathing, that she might not disturb him; not a tear in her eye, her whole being wound up into an external calm which was so strangely unlike the tumult within. And she had forsaken him—left him to meet calamity without her support, without sympathy or aid! She had been immersed in the pleasures of the children, their expeditions, their amusements. She remembered, with a shudder, that it had been a little relief to get him away, to have their dance undisturbed. Their dance! Her heart swelled as if it would burst. She had been his faithful wife since she was little more than a child. All her life was his—she had no thought, no wish, apart from him. And yet she had left him to bear this worst of evils alone!

Mrs. Sandford dared not break the sacred calm by a sob or a sigh. She dared not even let the tears come to her eyes, lest he should wake and be troubled by the sight of them. What thoughts went through her mind as she sat there, not moving! Her past life all over, which, until that telegram came, had seemed the easy tenor of every day; and the future, so dark, so awful, so unknown—a world which she did not understand without him.

After an interval he began to speak again, but so that she saw he was either asleep still or wandering in those vague regions between consciousness and nothingness. "All against the wall—with the faces turned," he said. "Three—all the last ones: the one my wife liked so. In the inner room: Daniells is a good fellow. He spared me the sight of them outside. Three—that's one of the perfect numbers—that's—I could always see them: on the road and on the moor, and at the races: then—I wonder—all the way up—on the road to heaven? no, no. One of the angels—would come and turn them round—turn them round. Nothing like that in the presence of God. It would be disrespectful—disrespectful. Turn them round—with their faces—" He paused; his eyes were closed, an ineffable smile came over his mouth. "He—will see what's best in them," he said.

After this for a time silence reigned, broken only now and then by a word sometimes unintelligible. Once his wife thought she caught something about the "four square walls in the new Jerusalem," sometimes tender words about herself, but nothing clear. It was not till night that he woke, surprising them with an outcry as to the light, as he had previously spoken about the darkness.

"You need not," he said, "light such an illumination for me—al giorno as the Italians say; but I like it—I like it. Daniells—has the soul of a prince." Then he put out his hands feebly, calling "Mary! Mary!" and drew her closer to him, and whispered a long, earnest communication; but what it was the poor lady never knew. She listened intently, but she could not make out a word. What was it? What was it? Whatever it was, to have said it was an infinite satisfaction to him. He dropped back upon his pillows with an air of content indescribable, and silent pleasure. He had done everything, he had said everything. And in this mood slept again, and woke no more.

Mr. Sandford's previsions were all justified. The house was sold to advantage, at what the agent called a fancy price, because it had been his house—with its best furniture undisturbed. Everything was miserable enough indeed, but there was no humiliation in the breaking up of the establishment, which was evidently too costly for the widow. She got her pension at once, and a satisfactory one, and retired with her younger children to a small house, which was more suited to her circumstances. And Lord Okeham, touched by the fact that Sandford's death had taken place under the same roof, in a room next to his own (though that, to be sure, in an age of competition and personal merit was nothing), found somehow, as a Cabinet Minister no doubt can if he will, a post for Harry, in which he got on just as well as other young men, and settled down into a very good servant of the State. And Jack, being thus suddenly sobered and called back to himself, and eager to get rid of the intolerable thought that he, too, had weighed upon his father's mind, and made his latter days more sad, took to his profession with zeal, and got on, as no doubt any determined man does when he adopts one line and holds by it. The others settled down with their mother in a humbler way of living, yet did not lose their friends, as it is common to say people do. Perhaps they were not asked any longer to the occasional "smart" parties to which the pretty daughters and well-bred sons of Sandford the famous painter, who could dispense tickets for Academy soirées and private views, were invited, more or less on sufferance. These failed them, their names falling out of the invitation books; but what did that matter, seeing they had never been but outsiders, flattered by the cards of a countess, but never really penetrating beyond the threshold?

Mrs. Sandford believed that she could not live when her husband was thus taken from her. The remembrance of that brief but dreadful time when she had abandoned him, when the children and their amusements had stolen her heart away, was heavy upon her, and though she steeled herself to carry out all his wishes, and to arrange everything as he would have had it done, yet she did all with a sense that the time was short, and that when her duty was thus accomplished she would follow him. This softened everything to her in the most wonderful way. She felt herself to be acting as his deputy through all these changes, glad that he should be saved the trouble, and that humiliation and confession of downfall which was not now involved in any alteration of life she could make, and fully confident that when all was completed she would receive her dismissal and join him where he was. But she was a very natural woman, with all the springs of life in her unimpaired. And by-and-by, with much surprise, with a pang of disappointment, and yet a rising of her heart to the new inevitable solitary life which was so different, which was not solitary at all, but full of the stir and hum of living, yet all silent in the most intimate and closest circle, Mrs. Sandford recognised that she was not to die. It was a strange thing, yet one which happens often: for we neither live nor die according to our own will and previsions—save sometimes in such a case as that of our painter, to whom, as to his beloved, God accorded sleep.

And more—the coming true of everything that he had believed. After doing his best for his own, and for all who depended upon him in his life, he did better still, as he had foreseen, by dying. Daniells sold the three pictures at prices higher than he had dreamed of, for a Sandford was now a thing with a settled value, it being sure that no new flood of them would ever come into the market. And all went well. Perhaps with some of us, too, that dying which it is a terror to look forward to, seeing that it means the destruction of a home, may prove, like the painter's, a better thing than living even for those who love us best. But it is not to every one that it is given to die at the right moment, as Mr. Sandford had the happiness to do.

THE WONDERFUL HISTORY OF MR. ROBERT DALYELL

CHAPTER I

It was a September night, rather chilly and dreary, as the evening often becomes at that season, even when the day has been beautiful. There was a little cold wailing wind about, like the ghost of an autumn breeze, which came in puffs of air, only strong enough to dislodge a fluttering yellow leaf or two, and sometimes with a few drops of rain upon it, which it dashed in your face with an elfish moan—not a night to walk in the garden for pleasure. It was, however, a custom with Mr. Dalyell to smoke his cigar out-of-doors after dinner in all weathers, and Fred, who was his eldest son, was proud to be his father's companion and share this indulgence—too proud to make any opposition to the chill of the night or the occasional dash of rain. All that was visible from the windows of the Yalton drawing-room, across which now and then a white figure would flutter, with a glance out were the red fire-tips of the two cigars, moving now quickly, now slowly, stopping altogether for a moment, going on with renewed rapidity—which was papa's way.

You could not see a prettier old house than Yalton in all the eastern shires. It had the mixture of French with native Scotch architecture which distinguishes a period in history. There were turrets, which the profane called pepper-boxes, at the corners, and lines of many windows in the commodious, comfortable corps de logis, now shining through the night with cheerful lights. Two terraces stood between the altitude of the house and the walk in which the father and son were, with lines of stone balustrades all overgrown by creeping plants and adorned with great vases in which the garish flowers of autumn were still fully blooming, though they were unseen in the darkness. On the lower level was the little temple of a fountain, which was reduced to a small and broken jet by age and negligence. The scent of the mignonette in the borders, the faint dripping of the water in the fountain, communicated to the atmosphere a little half-artificial speciality of character, like the terraces and great vases, not altogether natural to the locality, yet not uncongenial in its quaint double nationality. The two dark figures walking up and down, made visible by those red points, were yet undistinguishable, save by the fact that one was slim and slight, a boyish figure, and the other round and solid in the complete development of the man. The lad had been unfolding to his father the many novelties and wonders of his first year at the University, with that delightful force of conviction that such pleasant and wonderful experiences had never happened to anybody before which is the perennial belief of the young: while the father listened with that half-amused, half-pensive sympathy, made up of recollections fond and familiar, and the half-provoked, half-pleased sensation of amazement at finding those experiences re-embodied in the person of his son, which is habitual to the old. But, indeed, to say old is merely to express a comparative quality, for Mr. Dalyell of Yalton was a man under fifty, in the full force and vigour of life.

"Ah, yes," he said, "Fred, it's fine times for you now, my boy. But you must remember that life is not made up of bumps and bump-suppers, and that there are worse things than a proctor waiting for you, perhaps, round the next corner. I don't want you not to play—but you must learn to work a little, too."

"All right, father," said Fred; "I'll pull through. I sha'n't disgrace the old house."

"No," said Mr. Dalyell. "I don't suppose you will: but you might perhaps go a little farther than that."

"I didn't think," said Fred, surprised, "that you intended me to do more than a good pass. I never supposed there was—any need for hard work."

"Need? I never said there was need: but it does a young fellow good to be thought to work: even if it does no more it does that. It's well for you to be thought to work, Fred."

"If that's all," said the young man, "I don't fancy I want to get a reputation in that way."

"Then you're a silly boy," said his father. "It's a capital thing to have a good reputation. You don't know what it might do for you."

"Well," said the lad, with a laugh, "I don't fancy that matters so much, so long as you do everything for me, father."

"That's just the point, Fred. That's what I wanted to show you. I sha'n't always be here to do everything for you."

"Why," said Fred, "you're almost as young as I am!"

"I'm not particularly old: but no man's life is secure, however young he may be; it's not to be lippened to, as old Janet says. You ought to contemplate what your position would be if I were taken away. Think what happens to many a young fellow, Fred, whose father dies—perhaps just when he is where you are: and he has to stop all his pleasant ways and turn to, perhaps to work for his mother and the rest, perhaps only to look after them and take care of them—but at all events to be the head of the family instead of a careless boy." Mr. Dalyell had stopped in his walk to enforce what he said, which was a way he had. "I've known a boy of your age," he said, "that had to give up everything, and go into an office, and work like a slave: instead of your bump-suppers, Fred."

"I've heard of such a thing myself," said Fred; "though you don't think much of my experience, father. It happened to Surtees of New, a fellow a little senior to me. It was awfully hard upon him. He would have been in the 'eight' if he had stayed another year. What he felt most was leaving the 'Varsity without getting his blue. But," added the lad, "if it matters about what people think, as you were saying, he was thought no end of for it. He went abroad, I think, to look after some business there."

"And dropped, I suppose, never to be heard of more—among his old chums at least?"

"It was awfully hard upon him," said Fred, regretfully.

"Well," said Mr. Dalyell, "that's what may happen to any one of you whose fathers are in business. You ought to remember that such a contingency is always on the cards."

"Why, father—!" cried Fred. The boy was unwilling to make any application, to seem to think that there could be anything in their own circumstances to suggest this conversation: but he threw an involuntary glance at the house behind him with all its cheerful lights, and at the dark clouds of trees all round in the distance, which marked the great extent of the park and woods of Yalton. He did not add a word, and indeed the whole movement was involuntary—a sort of appeal from the lugubrious remarks on one side to all these unending signs of wealth on the other.

"You mean to say there's Yalton; and though I'm in business, I'm not all in business," said Mr. Dalyell with a laugh. "I was not speaking of ourselves, my boy; but of the vicissitudes of life. I hope there will be Dalyells of Yalton as long as Edinburgh Castle stands upon a rock; and one can't say more than that. Still, there are wonderful changes in life, and I'd like to think—if you force me to an application—that you were up to anything that might happen. You'd have to take the command, you know, Fred," he added after a moment, knocking the ash off his cigar against the balustrade of the terrace, with another curious laugh. "Your dear mother has never been used to anything but to be taken care of. You had better not bother her by asking advice from her if you should ever be in that position."

"I wish you would not say such dreadful things," said Fred petulantly. "Why should we talk of what I hope to heaven will never happen?—you make me quite uncomfortable, papa."

"Well, my dear boy," said Mr. Dalyell, "that's the penalty, don't you know, of being grown up—like shaving, and other disadvantages. You rather like the shaving—which implies an imaginary beard: but you don't like to hear of the much more important responsibilities."

"Shaving's inevitable," said Fred, giving a little furtive twirl to an almost imaginary moustache.

"Oh, is it?" said his father, with a more cheerful laugh. "Not for years yet; don't flatter yourself. When do you start for your ball to-morrow? It's fine to be an eligible young man, and sought after for all the dances. That's a pleasant consequence of being a 'Varsity man, and heir of Yalton, eh?"

"Well, father," said Fred, "seeing I've known the Scrymgeours all my life, we needn't put it on that ground. Whatever I was—if I was heir to nothing—it would be the same to them."

"Let's hope so," said Mr. Dalyell, and he breathed a sigh, which somehow got mingled with the little wail of the wind, and echoed into Fred's heart with a poignant suggestion. There was no reason to fear anything, and he was angry with himself. It was childish and superstitious to shiver as he did, as if the cold had caught him. There was no occasion in the world for anything of the sort. He was not a fellow to catch cold, he said to himself indignantly, nor to have presentiments, both of which things were equally absurd. There was nothing but prosperity and peace known in Yalton, and his father had the constitution of an elephant. But the night was eerie, the horizon had a sort of weird clearness upon it in the far distance, like a light showing through the openings of the clouds. The trees stood up black in billows of half-distinguishable shade, and the hills beyond them marked out their outlines wistfully against the clearness in the west. It was cold, and the air breathed of coming winter. A leaf drifting on the wind caught him on the cheek like a soft blow. Altogether the night was eerie, wild, full of possibilities. There was no ghost at Yalton; but sometimes old Janet said there was a sound in the avenue that meant trouble, like a horseman riding up to the house who never arrived. Fred involuntarily listened, as if he might have heard that horseman, which was as good as inviting trouble, but he did not think of that. However, there was no sound, nor ghost of a sound, except what was purely natural—the wild bitter wind wailing, driving a few leaves about, and bending, with a soft swish of the dark unseen foliage, the light branches of the trees.

"Come, let's go in, Fred; I've finished my cigar," said Mr. Dalyell; and then, as though a brain wave, as scientific people say, had passed from one to another—Fred's unspoken thought of old Janet suggested her to his father's mind. They were going up one of the sets of stone steps which led from one terrace to the other, when Mr. Dalyell suddenly put his hand on his son's arm:

"You'll laugh," he said, but not himself in a laughing tone, "at what I'm going to say. But if you should be in any difficulty what to do in case of my absence, or—or anything of that sort—do you know, Fred, whom I'd advise you to consult? The last person you would think of, probably, by yourself—old Janet! You know she's been about Yalton all her life. There's nothing she wouldn't do for any of us—and she's an extraordinarily sensible old woman, full of resource, and with a head on her shoulders—"

"I'm not fond of old Janet," said Fred sturdily.

"No, none of you are. Your mother never could be got to like her. It's a prejudice. She's been invaluable to me."

"If it's all the same to you, father," said Fred stiffly, "I'd rather not turn to an old wife for advice, an old nurse. What can she know? Of course your good opinion goes a very long way—"

"For or against? I'm afraid, so far as your mother is concerned, it is rather against. However, we need say no more about it. But, remember! as King Charles said."

They had paused on the landing between two flights of stairs. A great trail of yellow nasturtium, dropping from the vase at the corner, showed even in the dark a ghost of colour, and thrust its pungent odour into Fred's nostril. The faint billows of the trees stretched out dark and darker over the landscape below, and the cold clear light in the sky seemed to look on like a spectator who knows far more than the actors what is and is going to be. Fred once more gave a little shiver, and elevated his shoulders to his ears.

"You'd better go and take some camphor, boy. You've caught cold," his father said.

The drawing-room of Yalton was on the first floor, unlike the generality of country houses, which gave it a great advantage in respect to the landscape. On the ground floor a great deal of space was taken up with the hall, which opened into a large portico, and was scarcely light enough to be made much use of, in a climate where there is seldom too much sun. It happened, fortunately, that Mrs. Dalyell, who was a nervous and somewhat fantastic woman, was fond of a great deal of light, so that the large windows, which made the turreted Scotch house like a wing of the Louvre, were not displeasing to her. The curtains were but partially drawn over the central windows even now, so that it was possible to turn at any moment from the light and warmth of the interior to the wide landscape out-of-doors, with its wild breadth of sky and wailing winds. But within it was exceedingly bright with a number of lamps and candles and that pleasant blaze of a fire which it is an agreeable tradition in Scotch country houses to keep up in the evening, whether it is wanted or not. In September it is generally wanted; but it cannot be said there was any necessity for it on this particular night. The company in the drawing-room consisted of Mrs. Dalyell, her two daughters, and a gentleman of middle age and manners very ingratiating and friendly, if a little formal—Mr. Patrick Wedderburn, than whom no man was more respected in Edinburgh, a W.S. of the first eminence, learned in the law, and a favourite everywhere. He belonged, it need scarcely be said, to a good Scotch family, and was any man's equal in Scotland, though he acted as a "man of business" to many of his friends. He was one of the dearest friends of Robert Dalyell of Yalton, and was a more constant visitor than any other of the many familiar associates who called the laird of Yalton "Bob," and knew him and his affairs to the finger-points. Pat Wedderburn, as the visitor was commonly called, was an old bachelor, and therefore had no family to call him to a fireside centre of his own. He was as much in Yalton as he was in his own handsome but dull house in Ainslie Place, where, except when he had a dinner-party, the rooms were so silent, the solitude so serious. Neither the girls nor their mother made "company" of Mr. Wedderburn. He was seated in a deep chair, reading the papers while they talked, as if he were an uncle at the least, and he did not hesitate to interrupt their conversation now and then by reading out a bit of news or making a remark. He did not hesitate to correct Susie, who sometimes ventured upon a big word with which she was not familiar, and used it wrongly, or to tell Alice that she was a fidget, and could not keep still for five minutes; and as this was done from behind the newspaper, in the most accidental manner, it deepened still more the impression that nowhere could Mr. Wedderburn have been more perfectly at home. The papers, it may be added—that is to say, the London papers—arrived in Edinburgh in the evening. The conversation which was going on when Mr. Dalyell came into the drawing-room was, however, confined to the young people, and was chiefly on the subject of the Scrymgeour ball, to which Fred was going next day.

"I think they might have asked me," said Susie in an aggrieved tone. "I am just the same age as Lucy Scrymgeour. It isn't my fault mother, that you've never taken me out yet. I am seventeen and past, as everybody knows."

"No, it's not your fault. I am sure you have badgered me enough about it," said Mrs. Dalyell; "but though you think you can do anything you like with me, I have my opinions about some things. And one of them is that a girl should not go out too soon. People are quite capable of saying, ten or twenty years hence, 'Oh, Susie Dalyell, I can tell you her age to a day! She came out in such a year, and she must have been nineteen at the least.' That is exactly how people talk."

"And if they did," cries Susie, "what would it matter? Farmer thinks I look quite eighteen when I have my hair nicely dressed."

"That is all very well now, my dear; but wait till you are thirty or thirty-five. You would like to put on a year or two now, but you will like to take them off at the other end."

"Let's hope," said Mr. Wedderburn from behind his paper, "that she'll not be Susie Dalyell then."

"What difference will that make?" said Susie scornfully. "If I were forty I should never make a mystery about it. What is the use of trying to hide it, if you do have one foot in the grave?"

"Mother's forty—or more," said Alice, "and nobody would say she had one foot in the grave."

"Oh, what does it matter," cried Susie again, "at that time of life, when you are medeval and antediluvious? It is now that one minds."

"Susie, don't call mamma such dreadful names."

"Mediæval and antediluvian, Susie"—from behind the paper, in an undertone.

"I suppose," said Mrs. Dalyell tartly, "that Mr. Wedderburn thinks that quite appropriate. Gentlemen always think a girl's impertinence is amusing when it's directed against her mother; but you ought to know better, Susie, than to hold me up to ridicule. I am sure, whatever else I may be, I have been a careful mother to you."

"Oh, mamma! As if I meant anything like that," cried Susie petulantly, flinging herself upon her mother. "I only mean you don't care now. It's nothing to you to think of Lucy dancing all night in billows of tulle, like the girls in the novels, and me going to bed at ten o'clock. They will only just have begun then. And to think they should have asked Fred! and me Lucy's greatest friend and contemporaneous, and friends with Davie all my life—and that they never thought of asking me—never even tried! Perhaps if they had asked me—and it's such an opportunity and such old friends—you would have let me go."

"I'll tell you what, Susie," said Fred, who had just come in; "I'll ride over to-morrow morning first thing and ask them to ask you. I dare say they will for my sake."

Susie looked at him for a moment with a flush of hope, and then her face clouded. "For your sake!" she said, with a sister's frank contempt. "If it's only for your sake, I'll stay at home. I am not a nobody like that. I'm Lucy Scrymgeour's oldest friend. If she doesn't of her own account—and Davie too," cried the girl with an access of indignation—"it's more than any one can bear!"

"I would never speak to one of them again," said Alice, "if it was me."

"And what good would that do?" cried Susie, with the tear still in her eye, turning upon her sister. "Lose the ball and a friend too! I suppose they had some reason. Perhaps there were too many girls already—else why should they ask Fred? Or, perhaps—— Yes, I'll speak to Lucy again, the first time I see her; but I shall be very dignified, and pretend that I didn't care a bit."

"But you couldn't if you tried; dignified, my dear—that would be rather difficult."

"Is there anything in the paper, Pat?" said Mr. Dalyell.

"Not much. But it's ill talking between a full man and a fasting. I've seen what there is, and you've not. Here's the Times. Munro's in for that place in the North."

"Bless my soul! and you call that nothing? Another firebrand, and as good as two lost in our majority. That's bad, Pat; that's bad."

"I never think anything of a bye-election. They're all in the nature of accidents. There's a good speech of Gladstone's at one of the Lancaster towns, and John Bright flaming on the side of peace like a house on fire."

"And he says there's nothing in the paper!" said Mr. Dalyell, as he dropped into an easy-chair in his turn with the great broad-sheet of the Times in his hand.

"When gentlemen begin talking politics," said Mrs. Dalyell, "I always think it is time for the ladies to retire. But you have begun early to-night. Are you going into town at your usual hour to-morrow, Robert? I hope you'll be home early, for, with Fred away, there will be no man but only the servants in the house."

"And what the worse will you be for that, Amelia? There are plenty to protect you, I hope, if I were never to be seen again."

"Robert! that's not a thing to joke about. I never feel safe, you know, in this big, rambling old house when you're not here—if it was only the rats——"

"What could the rats do to you, mother?"

"Hold your peace, Fred!" said Mrs. Dalyell. "I sometimes think of Bishop Hatto in that poem you used all to be so fond of—and those in the Pied Piper. If you just heard some of old Janet Macalister's stories, they would make your hair stand on end."

"You'll be back in time, Bob, not to keep her uneasy," said Mr. Wedderburn behind the Standard, which he had just taken up, to his friend behind the Times.

Dalyell answered carelessly, "Yes, yes. Why shouldn't I be back in time?" Then, with a laugh, to his wife, "You should never mind old Janet. I dare say you were interfering with some hiding-holes of hers that she did not want disturbed. She's a kind of familiar spirit of the house, that old woman. She knows it better than any of us; and there's all sorts of uncanny corners about this house. It would be to keep you out of the secret chamber that she told you daft stories about the rats."

"I don't believe in any nonsense about secret chambers," said Mrs. Dalyell. "That's all very well in Glamis, and such places: but Yalton's not good enough for that."

"Yalton's good enough for anything, mamma," cried Susie, indignant. "I heard the horseman in the avenue a week ago, as clear as—"

"What's that you're saying, Susie?" said Mr. Dalyell sharply.

"Oh!" said the girl tremulously, "I mean the rain pattering in that place, you know."

"Susie is always hearing some nonsense," said her mother. "Gather up your work and things, children, for it is time you were going to your beds."

CHAPTER II

Mr. Wedderburn went into Edinburgh by the early train, the train which conveyed all the gentlemen who were business men. But Mr. Dalyell, who was not exactly a man in business, went in later. He had a great deal to do with that busy world, but he was not actually in harness with an office which claimed his daily attention. He was a director of a railway company, and he had something to do with a great insurance office, and there were other more speculative concerns in which he was believed to have an interest: and there were few days in the week in which he did not go "in," as everybody said, to Edinburgh; but still it was not a matter of necessity. He was up earlier than his wont that morning—for Yalton was not an early house in general—and "pottered about," as his wife said fretfully, from his dressing-room to the library and from the library back to his dressing-room, disturbing her morning's rest. He seemed to have a quantity of little things to do. Even after the breakfast bell had rung he ran twice into the library for something which he said he had forgotten. "You seem to have as many things to remember as if you were the Prime Minister," said Mrs. Dalyell, who had already poured out his coffee, and who was more annoyed when he left his breakfast to get cold than by any other of his peccadilloes. "Robert!" she cried from the door in a tone of exasperation, "there will be nothing fit to eat!" "I am coming, I am coming!" he cried. The curious thing was that he did not mind if his bacon was cold: but his wife minded for him and fumed and fretted. "What is the use of trying to get anything comfortable for your father?" she would say complainingly, "Well, mother, I like my kidneys hot," said Fred; "so they're not thrown away at least." Mrs. Dalyell looked at her son as if his tastes were a matter of much indifference, but softened when she met the lad's good-humoured blue eyes. He was not remarkable in appearance, but like dozens of other Scotch lads all about—light-brown hair, curling so strongly that it was difficult sometimes to comb it out; nice eyes, with a smile in them; tolerable features, the nose turned up a little; not a giant by any means, but well developed, well set up—a natural, pleasant boy of twenty, not without his failings, and perhaps a little careless, a little superficial, having had no occasion as yet to fathom any of the depths of life. He nodded at her over the dish of kidneys with a smile which was contagious. Mrs. Dalyell was by no means a light-hearted person. She was easily put out. She did not like anybody to have a different way of thinking from her own on the points that interested her. To let your tea stand till it was cold was an offence to Mrs. Dalyell. As for more serious matters she did not much interfere with them. That was the gentlemen's part of the business. To have breakfast in good condition and attend to the comfort of the house was hers, which perhaps is a view of the question which will commend itself to many. In return for this she expected to have a great deal of the trouble of life taken off her shoulders. She declared constantly that she knew nothing of business. She preferred to get her money just when she wanted it, instead of having a banking account of her own, as most ladies like to have nowadays, or a settled allowance. In short, Mrs. Dalyell was a woman whose very existence necessitated a husband behind her to do the rough work and see to the supplies. Within these limits there could not be a better mistress of a household. And she was exceedingly annoyed when her husband allowed his breakfast to get cold. It was a trick of his, of which it was her constant effort to mend him; but he was seldom so bad as this day.

"Go and tell your father," she said at last, "that it is almost time for the train. And to let him go without his breakfast is what I will not do. So just tell him, once for all, if he does not come at once he must just give up all thoughts of going in to Edinburgh to-day."

"Here I am—here I am, Amelia," said Mr. Dalyell, running in and taking his seat at table. "What have you got there, Fred? Kidneys!—and this is bacon."

"All just as cold as chucky-stones," said the lady of the house solemnly.

"You know I don't mind, my dear. I'll have a little of that kidney—and a cup of coffee with plenty of milk. How often am I to tell you you should never mind me?"

"Just as often as I tell you I will mind you, Robert. Who should be minded if it's not the master of the house?"

He cast upon her a look—which Fred, who had nearly but not quite forgotten the conversation of last night, caught and wondered at with a vague sense of pain, though his mother did not remark it. There was a great deal of affection and tenderness in the glance; but something else that puzzled him. There was trouble in it—but what trouble could there be in his father's eyes looking at his mother? There was something in it which made him say quite inconsequently, looking up from his plateful of devilled kidney, "You're not going away anywhere, are you, father?"

Then his father's eyes fixed on himself with a startled glance: "Away?" he said. "Where should I be going? and what's put that into your head?"

Fred replied with the familiar subterfuge of youth: "Oh, nothing!" But his mind was not satisfied; for that was no answer. And there passed through his thoughts a vague idea that if, later in the day, there came a telegram saying that Mr. Dalyell had been obliged to go to London on business, he would not be surprised.

"Where indeed!" said Mrs. Dalyell. "It's not the time for business, which is a comfort: for you can't be running up to London at a moment's notice, as you did in the spring. You would find nobody there."

"That is just it," said Mr. Dalyell. And after he had made this unquestioned observation, he added, "I shall perhaps run down to Portobello and get a swim. Nothing puts a man right like the sea. I'll just take a plunge and be back by the four o'clock train."

"I hope you'll have somebody with you; and don't you be too venturesome with your plunging and your swimming."

"Too venturesome on Portobello sands! I'll get Pat Wedderburn to come and look after me," said Mr. Dalyell with a laugh. He laughed with his lips, but his eyes were quite grave—which was all the more remarkable since he had laughing eyes, with humorous puckers all about them, exceedingly ready to light up at such a joke as that of being taken care of by Pat Wedderburn. He had still half-a-dozen things which kept him running out and in before he was ready to start, which his way, but always a source of exasperation to his orderly wife. Finally, when there was hardly time to catch the train, he dashed upstairs three steps at a time, explaining that he had forgotten something. Mrs. Dalyell stood wringing her hands at the open door.

"I wish you had ordered the dog-cart, Fred. He'll never catch the train. You should remember your father's ways, and that this is always what happens: and then he'll just fly and get out of breath and over-heated—the very worst things for him. Dear, dear me! I might have had more sense. I might have ordered the dog-cart myself, there's only ten minutes—"

"If he does lose the train I suppose it won't matter so much," said easy-minded Fred.

"Not if he would think so," replied the mother, "nothing at all—but when he sets his mind on a thing, possible or impossible, he will carry it out. ROBERT!" she cried, in capitals, going to the bottom of the stairs.

"I'm coming, I'm coming!" he shouted. His voice came not from the direction of his room but from the west passage, where he had nothing to do, a fact which awoke a vague surprise in Mrs. Dalyell's mind. He came downstairs "like a tempest," she said afterwards, making as much noise, and caught her in his arms, to her great astonishment. "Good-bye, my dearest, good-bye!" he cried, giving her a loving kiss ("before the bairns, and that man Foggo looking on!"). "Keep well and don't distress yourself about me." He was gone almost before she could ask him why she should distress herself about him, flying down the road with Fred after him, which, indeed, was his usual way of catching a train. She stood at the door looking after him, and though he was in such a hurry and not a moment to lose, what did Robert do but turn round and take off his hat and wave his hand to her! Such nonsense! as if he were going away for years. She made a sign of impatience, hurrying him on. "Do you think they will do it this time, Foggo?" she said to the butler, who was also looking after them. Foggo had been standing ready to help his master on with his coat. But Mr. Dalyell had time only to snatch it and throw it over his shoulder, partly because of that unnecessary embrace which had so confused his wife under the servant's eyes.

"Oh, ay, ma'am," said Foggo, "they'll do it; the maister's aye just on the edge—but he's never missed her yet—"

Mr. Dalyell, when he rushed upstairs, had not gone to his dressing-room as he proposed to do. He had darted down the west passage, a long vacant corridor with a few doors of unused bedrooms on one side. He went down to the end room of all, and opened the door. An old woman in a tremendous mutch and tartan shawl came forward to meet him. "I have come to say good-bye, Janet, my woman," he said, grasping her hand. "And you'll remember what you've promised."

"That I will, my bonnie man: if you're sure you must do it. As long as I live—but then I, may be, have not very long to live."

"We'll have to trust for that," he said, holding both her hands.

"Could you no trust for other things? I've preachit to ye till I'm weariet, maister Robert! Nobody trusted yet and was disappointed."

"We've gone over all that," he said. "No, no, there's no other way. We can't ask the Lord for money, Janet."

"What for no? And now I can scarce say God's blessing on ye—for how can I ask His blessing when it's for a—?"

"No more, Janet, no more. Good-bye!"

"Oh, maister Robert, bide a moment. Do you mind the Psalm:

'If in your heart ye sin regard The Lord you will not hear?'

Think of that! How can I bid Him bless ye, when—?"

"Good-bye, my dear old woman, good-bye!"

And it was at this moment that Mrs. Dalyell's voice calling "Robert!" came small in the distance up the echoing passage. And in another moment he was gone.

Mrs. Dalyell went to her kitchen to give her orders to the cook as soon as her husband was out of sight. She was an excellent housekeeper, and enjoyed this part of her duties far too much to depute them to any other, although indeed in the tide of prosperity which Mr. Dalyell's business had brought to Yalton she might have had a housekeeper had she pleased, and a much larger establishment. But she had thrifty instincts and that distrust of business which old-fashioned ladies used to have, with an inward conviction that it always collapsed at one time or another, and that the estate was the sheet-anchor: which had prevented her ever from launching out into expense. She dismissed the thoughts of Robert's unusual embrace—for domestic endearments are sedulously kept in the background in Scotch houses of the old-fashioned type—and of any little peculiarity there might have been about him this morning more than other mornings—from her mind: which it required no effort to do, for she was not given to investigations below the surface, or reading between the lines, and a parting kiss (though absurd) was a parting kiss to Mrs. Dalyell, and it was nothing more. She took pains to order her husband a very good dinner, with due consideration of his special likings, which perhaps was as good a thing as she could have done. Then after luncheon there was Fred to send off in good time, so that he might not put out any of the Scrymgeours' arrangements by arriving too late. He had a seven-miles drive, and never would have recollected to order the dog-cart in time if his mother had not taken that duty upon herself; and she likewise cast a glance at his other arrangements to make sure that his white ties were in good condition and his pumps as they ought to be—precautions quite unnecessary and rather distasteful to the young man in his new conviction, acquired at Oxford, that he knew better than any one what was essential to a perfect turn-out, either for horse or man. Susie, who was liberated from lessons after luncheon, spent her time in preparing messages for Lucy Scrymgeour which were intended to disturb and plant thorns in that young person's mind. "You can tell her I never was so surprised in my life as when it came for you and not for me: for you never were such friends with them as me. But you're only asked as a man. They must be badly off for men; though when one thinks of all the officers in the garrison—and Davie such friends with all of them! I don't think you have got any amatory instincts, Fred—for you've no friends but Oxford men; and what good would they be to us if we had a ball? But you can tell Davie from me—"

"Has Davie amatory instincts?" cried Fred. "The little beast—I'll take him no messages from you."

"What on earth is the child talking of?" said Mrs. Dalyell. "Where did she hear such a word? Amatory!"

"It means friendship," cried Susie, with a burning blush. "I know—I know it does! I mean Davie has such lots of friends—and Fred has none; or at least none that would be of any use if we were to have a ball."

"But we are not going to have a ball," said the mother; "it is a great deal too much trouble. Ask the Scrymgeours what they think a week hence. The whole house will be turned upside down, and the servants put out of the way, and everybody made wretched. No, Susie, there will be no ball."

"Then am I never to come out at all?" said Susie in a voice from which consternation had driven all the lighter tones. This was too solemn a thought to be expressed except with the gravity of fate.

"You should present her, mother," said Fred; "that's the right thing for a girl."

"Oh, my dear," said Mrs. Dalyell, "that's a great trouble too! The gowns alone would cost about a hundred pounds; and your father, you know, never stays a day longer in London than he can help—and what would Susie and me do, two women by ourselves in that great big place? Besides, to make it worth the while we would need to know a number of people and get invitations. I've often heard of country people, very well thought of in their own place, that have just been humiliated to the very dust in London, with nobody to ask them out, or to call on them or anything. She'll have to be content with something nearer home."

"That is all because things are so conventional and nothing natural," said Susie; "that is what they say in all the books. But if papa would go up with us in his Deputy Lieutenant's uniform, and knowing such quantities and quantities of people—and perhaps if you were to tell Mrs. Wauchope she might speak to the Duchess, and the Duchess would say just a little word to one of the Princesses—and then perhaps the Queen—"

"Are you out of your senses, Susie? What do you expect that the Queen would do?"

"Well! they might say we belonged to D'yell of Yalton that saved the life of James the Fourth, who is the Queen's great, great, great (I don't know how many greats) grandfather. And if she was passing this way, you know, mamma, my father would have to come out and offer her a drink of milk upon his knees. And it is a real old rule for thousands of years, a feudacious tenor, or something of that kind—"

"Where did you find all that, Susie? Is it true, mother? Do we hold Yalton like that?" cried Fred in great delight. "I never knew we were such distinguished people before."

"I don't see any distinction about it," said Mrs. Dalyell: "I never paid much attention to such old stories. Oh, if you believe all the Dalyell stories— By the way, Susie, I wish you to pronounce the name as I do— as everybody is doing now. 'D'yell' is so common—it is what the ploughmen say."

"It is the right old antiquous way," said Susie with energy, "and I like it far the best. I heard about the horseman too—what it means," she added in a low tone. "Papa will never let me speak, but I could tell you such things, Fred, if—" And here the little girl made various telegraphic signs, meaning that enlightenment might be afforded if they were alone together, with the mother well out of the way. These designs, however, were frustrated unconsciously by Mrs. Dalyell, who gave her daughter something to do in the way of replying to notes, which kept Susie busy until it was time for Fred to depart.

But yet there was a little time for talk when the girls went with him round to the stables to remind the groom that he must not be late.

"Where did you hear about that feudal business, Susie?" said Fred. "Did you get it out of a book?"

"I got it out of something much funnier. I got it out of old Janet. You should just hear her; she knows more about us—oh! so much more—than we know about ourselves. She told me about—"

"Old Janet!" said Fred. He had forgotten his father's grave talk and all that had passed on the terrace, and it was not till he had thought it over for a minute or two that it slowly came back to him what association that was which was linked with the name of old Janet. Not that he had not perfect acquaintance with her, as a matter of fact. She had been Mr. Dalyell's nurse, and had always possessed a room of her own at Yalton, where she lived in a curious isolation and independence—respected, and, perhaps, a little feared by the household in general. Fred endeavoured to remember what it was as Susie's voice ran on, and then it suddenly burst upon him. It was to her his father had advised him to go if he wanted help, in the supposed contingency of his own removal—old Janet, of all people in the world! The recollection made Fred indignant, yet gave him a sort of shiver of alarmed presentiment as well. Could his father have meant anything more than a mere passing fancy? Yet surely he must have meant something. And under what possible circumstances could he, Fred, a University-man, and acquainted with the world, require to take counsel with old Janet? It gave him the strangest thrill to his very finger-points. It must mean something different from what it seemed to mean. His father would never have given him such a recommendation without a reason. Fred thought with a sensation of horror of the family secrets which such an old woman might possess. She might know something that would ruin them all—there might be something hanging over them, something which she had to break to him. Fred flung this fancy out of his mind as if it had been a stone that some one had thrown into it, and came back to what Susie was saying. Indifferent to the fact that he was not listening, Susie was recounting the story of the family warning.

"'And since that time there has always been a sound in the avenue as if some horseman was coming, heavy dunts on the road, and the tinkle of the bridle,' she says. Always when there is trouble coming. I am sure it must be very fatiguing for a ghost, and monotonious—oh! just beyond description—to ride that little bit of road and never come near the house, and all just to frighten a person. I would dash into the hall and shake my bridle at them if it was me."

"If you were a ghost, Susie?" said Alice with a shiver. "Oh, how can you think of yourself as a ghost?"

"I don't: I'm not diaphanious," said Susie; "but if you were to be a ghost at all it would be better to have something more to do than just dunting, dunting, over one bit of road."

"Janet must have been telling you a lot of lies and nonsense," said Fred indignantly; "I'll have to speak to her if she goes on like that."

"Or tell papa," said Alice. "He never likes to hear about the horseman."

"Yes, or tell papa," said Fred. He could not tell what it meant, but he had a strange feeling as if it were he himself that must do this and shield his sisters from things that might frighten them—as if his father somehow had not much to do with it. But he was greatly shocked with himself when he became conscious of this thought. He was so much absorbed, indeed, in the uncomfortable fancies called up by Janet's name, that Susie's story of the King's hunting and danger of his life, and how the goodwife of Yalton brought him a bowl of milk, and how the lands, as much as they could ride round in a day, according to the most approved romantic fashion, were bestowed upon the D'yells for that service, had little effect upon her brother. And presently the dog-cart came round to the door, and the sight of Fred seated in it with his portmanteau diverted Susie's thoughts also and brought back her grievance. She stood watching his departure by the side of her mother, who had come out as was her wont to see the boy off.

"There he goes!" said Susie. "Oh, what fossilized hearts boys have! He never thinks of me that has to stay at home. Tell Lucy Scrymgeour if she thinks I will ask her to our ball she is in the greatest mistake, and it will be just as much splendider than theirs, as Yalton is better than Westwood. And tell her mamma is going to take me to London to be presented and make my three obeysances to the Queen, and when I have done that I can go to every place, and all the other queens are obliged to ask me. Well, if mamma doesn't, it's not my fault; but you can always tell her, Fred: and just say to that ichthyosaurious Davie that I'll have all the grand guardsmen and equerries to talk to, and I wouldn't look at him."

"But it's not his fault, Susie," said Alice; "and perhaps he'll tell Fred he is very sorry."

"I don't think he will, for boys have no hearts: they have vegetable things instead, when they are not fossilized. If he says he is sorry, Fred, you can say I don't mind very much, only I'll never speak to them again."

"I hope you'll have a nice ball, Fred," said Mrs. Dalyell. "Come back as early as you can to-morrow, for there are some people coming to tea. And you may bring over Lucy and David, and any other young ones that are staying at Westwood. We can give them their tea on the terrace, it's not too cold for that; and I am sure Mrs. Scrymgeour will be thankful to any one that will take them out of her way."

CHAPTER III

About the time when Fred was starting from Yalton Mr. Wedderburn, the friend of the family, might have been seen in his office in a condition very unlike his usual calm. That he was very much disturbed about something was evident. His table was covered with all those carefully-arranged letters and docketed papers which are essential to the pose of a man of business; and by intervals he wrote a letter—or, rather, part of a letter—to which he added a line whenever he could fix his thoughts to it; but these intervals were scattered through the reflections and calculations of several hours, to which Mr. Wedderburn returned, from minute to minute, laying down his pen and falling back into some more absorbing subject of thought. Sometimes he got up and walked about the room, going from one window to the other, and staring out at each as if the slight variation of the view could afford him some light upon the subject over which he puckered his brows. Now and then he said to himself audibly, "I must go out to-night." He was not a man who indulged in the habit of speaking to himself, nor was there much in these words which could throw light upon the subject of his thoughts; but it was evidently a sort of relief to him to say this as he paced heavily about the room and looked out, staring blankly, neither seeing, nor expecting to see, anything that would clear up the trouble on his face. "I must go out to-night." This phrase, however, meant a great deal to the sober and reserved Edinburgh lawyer.

It meant that to the house which he visited so often, receiving hospitality, kindness, and a sense of almost family well-being, for which he gave back nothing but a steady, undemonstrative friendship, the moment had now come when he must go in another character—in the character, indeed, of an anxious brother and helper, but yet as announcing an approaching catastrophe and the breaking-up of a superstructure of long-established prosperity and peace. He had not been convinced of the necessity of this till to-day. Whispers, indeed, had come to his ears of doubtful speculations and a position which was beginning to be assailed by questions which never should arise as to the position of a man in business. But he had lent a deaf ear to all that was malicious, and brushed away all friendly fears. "Bob D'yell's as sensible a fellow as ever stepped. It'll take strong evidence to make me believe that he's been playing ducks and drakes with his money." This confident speech from a man of Pat Wedderburn's authority (in Edinburgh, as in fashionable circles, the well-known members of the community are generally distinguished by their Christian names) had done much to support a credit which was not so robust as it had been. But this morning Mr. Wedderburn had heard very unpleasant things—things which had gone to his heart, and wounded both his affection and his pride. He had a pride in his friend's credit as in his own. And when he thought of the cheerful household and all its innocent indulgences, Mr. Wedderburn struck the table with his fist in the trouble of his heart. To think that they might have to leave Yalton, to give up their little luxuries, their social rank, all the pleasures of their life, affected this old bachelor as probably it would not at all affect themselves. He could have shed angry tears over the "putting down" of Mrs. Dalyell's carriage and the girls' ponies, which, if it came to that, and they were aware that their position required such sacrifices, these ladies would give up without a murmur; and, perhaps, none of them would have much objection to come "in" to a house in Edinburgh instead of Yalton, which was a possibility which made Mr. Wedderburn swear. He was very unhappy about them, one and all, and about his life-long friend, Bob D'yell, who must no doubt have been in the wrong, and whom sometimes in his heart he blamed angrily and bitterly, thinking what the effect of his rashness would be to the others. Pat Wedderburn was grieved to the heart. He could as easily have believed in himself going wrong; "But, God bless us!" he said to himself, "it's not going wrong. He has been taken in; he was always a sanguine fellow, and he's been deceived." His thoughts finally resolved themselves into the necessity, above and before all things, of having a long talk with Bob; and he repeated, as he once more stared mechanically out of the further window, "I must go out to-night."

He could not, however, go "out" before the usual time, and in the interval he could not rest. Finally, he took his hat and left his office with a better inspiration. If he could find his friend at one of the establishments in which he had an interest, the talk might be had at once, without any need, at least for to-night, of disturbing the peaceful echoes of Yalton. Mr. Wedderburn went out for this purpose with very tender thoughts of his friend mingled with his anger. "Why couldn't the fellow tell me in time? But the Lord grant it may still be in time! There's things I might have done. I'm not without funds nor resources, nor ideas, either, for that matter." And as Mr. Wedderburn went along the orderly Edinburgh street, he burst out into a kind of laugh, such as is among many elderly Scotchmen the last evidence of emotion, and said within himself: "To the half of my kingdom!" The humour of the contrast between that romantic phrase and the very prosaic, rapid calculation he had gone through as to the money he— not a romantic person at all, an Edinburgh W.S., of fifty-five, and of the most humdrum appearance— could command: and the true feeling with which he had realised his friend's misfortune, burst forth in that anomalous sound. A woman who was passing turned round and looked at him with puzzled alarm; and a boy, one of those rude commentators who spare nobody's feelings, called out, "That's a daft man; he's laughing to himsel'." "Laughing," said Mr. Wedderburn with something like a groan: "there is little laughing in my head." And so he went on to the Railway Office, and the Insurance Office, to ask for Mr. Dalyell.

At the railway he had not been seen that day, at the other office he had appeared for about half an hour only.

"He will have returned home, I suppose," Wedderburn said indifferently.

"Well, no, sir; not at once," said the clerk who answered his questions. "I heard him saying he was feeling fagged, and that he was going out to Portobello for a dip in the sea and a good swim."

"It's a little cold for that," said Wedderburn.

"Well, it may be a little cold," admitted the clerk cautiously, "but Mr. D'yell is a great man for the sea."

"He will probably be going out by the usual train," Mr. Wedderburn said to himself as he turned away. But there was no appearance of Dalyell in the train. The lawyer walked to Yalton through the cornfields, in which the harvest had begun, just as the sun was sinking. The ruddy autumnal light came into his eyes, half blinding him with its long, level rays. Everything was rosy with the brilliancy of the sunset; the blue sky flushed with ruddy clouds, the warm colour of the sheaves catching a still warmer tone from the sun. All was peaceful, wealthy, full of external comfort and riches, and the house of Yalton caught the sinking gleams from the west upon its high roof and pinnacles like a benediction. The trees were taking the autumn livery here and there, giving as yet only a little additional warmth to the landscape. To go from Yalton to Melville Street, or some other dread abode of stony gentility in Edinburgh, how could they ever bear it? Mr. Wedderburn had been going over all his resources as he made his little journey, and he had reckoned up what he could spare to set his friend on his legs again. Perhaps there might yet be time!

When he went into the drawing-room where Mrs. Dalyell was sitting, she raised her head from her work, with a smile on her face. And then he observed a little alteration—oh, not so much as a cloud upon her face, not even a look that could be called disappointment, but only the slightest scarcely perceptible change of expression. "Mr. Wedderburn!" she said. "I'm very glad to see you: but I thought it was Robert," and she held out her hand to him with all the easy confidence of habitual friendship. She was not disappointed; there was no doubt in her mind that Robert was coming, if not behind his friend, at least with the next train.

"You will be surprised to see me so soon again," he said, feeling a little embarrassed. "You will think you are never to be quit of that old fellow—but I wanted to have a long talk with Bob on some business; and as I could not find him at the office—"

"No," said Mrs. Dalyell; "he said as soon as he could get his business over he was going down to Portobello for a dip in the sea. I never knew such a man for the sea. No doubt that has made him lose his train—for he's generally very punctual by this train."

"That is what I thought," said Mr. Wedderburn. "I thought I would meet him and come out with him. But the next will bring him, no doubt."

"In about three-quarters of an hour," said Mrs. Dalyell, calmly: and she added, "It's a beautiful evening, and it's a pity to keep you in the house. We should take the good of the fine weather as long as it lasts. Never mind me: you will find the girls upon the terrace somewhere. But take a cup of tea before you go out."

"I will take a cup of tea," said the visitor, "thankfully. But why not come out upon the terrace yourself? It is the most lovely afternoon, and the wind, as much as there is, is from the west. It's a sin to stay in the house when you have such a place to see the sunset from. Now if you were in Melville Street, for instance—"

"Why Melville Street?" said Mrs. Dalyell with a laugh—but she did not wait for an answer. "If I had to live in Edinburgh I would never go there. I would prefer the south side—or old George's Square where the houses are so good. I sometimes think we will have to come in for the winter now that Susie's of an age for parties, for there is little gaiety for a young thing here."

"That's true," said Mr. Wedderburn, and he gave her a look in which there was an inquiry and a moment's doubt. Did she perhaps know something? Had Bob D'yell confided some hint of approaching calamity or necessary retrenchment to the wife of his bosom? What so natural, what so wise? Mrs. Dalyell's head was a little bent over the table where she stood pouring out a cup of tea for the visitor; but she raised it, meeting that inquiring look with the perfect frankness of her usual demeanour and the calm of a woman round whom there had never been any mysteries. She was struck, however, by his look. "Is there anything the matter?" she said. "You are looking very serious." Then, for heaven knows what womanish reason, it occurred to her that Mr. Wedderburn was himself in trouble, and wanting something of her husband. "You know," she said with a little emphasis, "that whatever might be the matter, if there's anything that Robert could do, Mr. Wedderburn, you are as sure of him as of a brother." "God bless her innocence!" the lawyer said to himself.

"Not a bit," he said. "There's nothing the matter: but thank you all the same for saying that. Bob D'yell's been to me as a brother, since we were boys together—and will be I hope till the end."

Mrs. Dalyell put out her soft hand to him over the tea-table with a smile. There was water in his eyes, though, fortunately, as he stood with his back to the light, it could not be seen—but there was none in hers. Her eyes were as serene as the evening skies; and her soft hand, which perhaps was a little too soft, with no bones in it to speak of, the hand of a woman never used to do much for herself, met his strong grasp, in which there was more than many an oath of fidelity, with a moderate and simple kindness which showed at once how natural and genuine was the friendship to which she thus pledged her husband, and how devoid of all tragical elements so far as her comprehension went. She was a little surprised by Mr. Wedderburn's grip, which rather hurt that soft hand, but led the way to the terrace, after he had taken his tea, with all her usual serenity. She took a shawl from the stand in the hall and wrapped herself in it as she went out. In Scotland even in July it is wise to take a shawl when you go out to see the sunset; how much more in September! Indeed, after she had taken two or three turns upon the terrace, she went in again, saying that it was all very well for "you young things" (with a smile at Mr. Wedderburn), but that she knew what rheumatism was. Susie and Alice were very good company on the terrace, and they had a thousand things to say to their old friend, so that, though he had looked occasionally at his watch, he had not taken very decided note of the passage of time, until an hour after, when Mrs. Dalyell came back again, with a shawl this time over her head. The sun had quite gone down, the shadows were lengthening, and twilight stealing on. "Do you mean to say," Mrs. Dalyell said as she came down the steps to the terrace, "that your father's not here? I made sure he must be here with you: the train's been in this half-hour, and there's not another till nine—and no telegram. I don't know what it can mean."

It could not be said, perhaps, that she was anxious, but she was uneasy, not knowing what to think. Mr. Wedderburn, for his part, started, as if the fault had somehow been his. "Bless me!" he said, "I had forgotten all about it. I might have gone down and met the train."

"That would have done little good," said Mrs. Dalyell, "for if he had come by it he would have been here before now: the thing that astonishes me is there's no telegram. Sometimes Robert, like other people, is detained. Every business man must be detained now and then: but he always sends a telegram. I never knew him to fail."

"That is the worst," said Mr. Wedderburn, "of being too exact in your ways. If you ever depart from them by any accident everybody thinks something must have happened."

"I don't think something must have happened," said Mrs. Dalyell, "but I don't understand it. It's so unlike him. He would rather take any trouble than keep me anxious; and I told him particularly we should be alone to-night, with no man except servants in the house. It's not like Robert. It must have been something quite unforeseen."

"Such things are always happening, my dear lady. He may have had to meet some man from London; he may even have had to go to London himself."

"Dear me!" said Mrs. Dalyell, "you don't think that's likely? Without so much as a clean shirt! Besides, he would have sent a telegram," she repeated, going back to the one thing of which she was sure.

"It's the telegram you miss more than the man," said Mr. Wedderburn with a laugh. It was very very little of a laugh. He was more miserable than she, for her anxiety was quite unmixed by any deeper sense of a possible reason for her husband's absence. There was no reason for it, none whatever to her consciousness.

"That is just it. I want the telegram to explain the man. Of course, he might be called away. Would I have him tied to my apron-string? But a word of warning, that's what I look for. 'Kept by business and will not be back till the late train,' or 'Dining at the Lord President's,' or—it does not matter what it is. I am always glad that Robert should enjoy himself, so long as I have my telegram. But as it's evident he's not coming," said Mrs. Dalyell, looking at her watch, "we must just take our dinner and hope he's getting as good a one. He will be coming by the nine train."

Mr. Wedderburn went in with very painful fancies, which he could not shake off. The moment would have come, perhaps, when Bob D'yell had to tell his family that he was a ruined man, and he would be shrinking from that stern necessity. His friend pictured him wandering about the dark streets, or sitting in the rooms above the Insurance Office, where there was space to receive on occasion a belated director, and counting up all he had—alas! would it not rather be all the debts he had—reckoning them, and asking himself how long it would be before the storm burst, and how he was to tell her, and what the poor children would do? That was what the poor fellow would be thinking, wherever he was. Instead of coming back—the good lawyer exclaimed within himself in a little attempt at anger, to keep his sympathy from becoming too heart-rending—to one that might have helped him! But that would be just like Bob D'yell—ready enough to come to you if you were in trouble, to give all his mind to what was to be done: but not if the trouble was his own: more likely then to hide himself, to think shame of it, as if misfortune was a man's own fault. Mr. Wedderburn did not know what to do, whether to hurry into Edinburgh to make inquiries, or to wait on, and see whether he would arrive by the late train. Somehow he had very little faith that his friend would come home. He might go away, thinking, perhaps, that the creditors would be more gentle with his family if he were gone. And that would be called absconding! Heaven only could tell what in his despair the poor fellow might do.

Except suicide: there never occurred to his friend, in the endless thoughts he had on the subject, any fear of that, which to a Frenchman would be the first thing to be thought of—the natural refuge for a bankrupt. No, no!—come what might there was no need to think of that dark contingency. Besides, Mr. Wedderburn reflected, with a sense of the grim humour of the suggestion, that Dalyell, as the director of an insurance company, knew too well that such a step would take away the last resource his children might have. No, no!—not that. But he might go away. He might not be able to bear the sight of ruin as affecting them. That was what chiefly weighed upon himself—the woman and her children; the girls, who would not know what it meant; and poor Fred, who would know what it meant—who would have to abandon everything on which his heart was most set. Had Wedderburn been aware of the conversation which had taken place between Fred and his father his troubled thoughts would have been still more serious: as it was, all he could do was to keep his countenance, to look as like his ordinary as possible, not to frighten the poor things too soon.

But the dinner went over well enough. Mrs. Dalyell kept looking at the door every time it opened, though she knew it was only to admit a new dish, expecting her telegram. But it did not come. And the nine o'clock train arrived, and there was still no appearance of the master of the house. The footman was sent down to meet the train, and Wedderburn put on his coat, and said shyly that he would just take a turn and meet the truant. And the girls ran out by the terrace, and one strayed down the avenue to bring papa home. And though it was cold, Mrs. Dalyell opened one of the drawing-room windows that she might hear him coming. She was not alarmed: but she was so much surprised that it made her a little uneasy, for in all her married life such a thing had never happened to her before.

When it proved that he had not come by the nine o'clock train nobody knew what to think. By this time the telegraph-office was closed at the village, and there was no longer any hope of news that way: which, strangely enough, was a thing that rather calmed than otherwise Mrs. Dalyell's mind.

"He must be coming by the midnight express," she said.

"Would you like me to go in and see if there was anything the matter?" said Mr. Wedderburn.

"What could be the matter?" she said.

"Oh, he might be ill—or there might have been an accident!"

"In that case," said Mrs. Dalyell, "Robert never would have omitted to send a telegram—or the people at the office, or wherever he was, would have done it. No, no! You would go in to Edinburgh anxious, and we could not let you know that he had got the express to stop. Just stay where you are. And we'll hear all about it when he comes. And it's a comfort to have you in the house."

To this request Mr. Wedderburn at once yielded. If the poor fellow did come home, miserable and disheartened, it was better that he should see a friend's face, and take counsel with a man who was ready to help and advise before he told her. Besides, it was better for her, poor thing, to have somebody to stand by her. And, oddly enough, now that there was no chance of that telegram she was not so anxious. She had no doubt of Robert coming by the express. She let Alice stay up beyond her bedtime to make up a rubber for Mr. Wedderburn, and took her share in the game quite cheerfully. She did not believe in either illness or accident. "He would have had no peace till I was by his bedside," she said; "and anybody could have sent a telegram." No, no, she had no fear of that: and expected now quite calmly the last train.

But Mr. Dalyell did not come by the midnight express.

CHAPTER IV

There is something dreadful in the aspect of a room from which its habitual occupant is absent unexpectedly all night. Its good order, its cold whiteness, the unused articles in tidy array, undisturbed by any careless natural movements, strike a chill to the heart. In any case, even when the usual tenant is pleasantly absent, or gone on a visit, there is something ominous in the empty room. It seems to breathe of a time when the familiar person will be gone for ever. And how much more when the beloved occupant has gone mysteriously—absent, lost in the unknown—no one knowing where he has passed the night! Mrs. Dalyell was not a fanciful woman, she was not given to morbid imaginations, but when she glanced into her husband's dressing-room next morning her heart sank for a moment with this chill, that would not be reasoned away. She did reason it away, however, and recovered her composure. For, after all, what was it?—nothing. A man in active life has a hundred calls upon him. He might be whipped off to London upon some railway business without any warning. The only thing that really troubled her was the absence of that telegram. It was still almost summer weather; nothing to interrupt the working of the telegraph anywhere. Already even she might have had one had he telegraphed from any station on the way up to London. This was the thing which she could not understand.

"No, there is no word," she said. "I have made up my mind he must have been called off at a moment's notice to London; but why he didn't telegraph, I can't imagine—even from Berwick he might have done it, and I should have had it by this time. I never knew Robert so careless before."

"Here it is, mother," cried Alice, rushing in with the famous yellow envelope, the hideous messenger of so much trouble. But when Mrs. Dalyell took it, she flung it back again almost with indignation, and turned upon the girl with a sort of fury.

"Couldn't you see," she cried, "that it was for Mr. Wedderburn?" The poor lady had kept her nerves quiet and her imagination suppressed till now. But this felt to her like an injury. She got up from the breakfast-table, and paced about the room, wringing her hands. It had come, but it was not for her! This seemed to put terror into the anxiety, an increase of every involuntary tremor. In the sickness of the disappointment tears came rushing to her eyes. She took Alice by the shoulders and gave her a shake. "Couldn't you see? you little careless monkey!" Poor Mrs. Dalyell was unjust in the heat of her disappointment. But after a while reason once more resumed its sway. "I am letting it get upon my nerves," she said with a tremulous laugh, as she came back to the table. Then, with a glance at Mr. Wedderburn's disturbed face, "It is not by any chance—about Robert?" she cried.

"No—no—I've no reason to suppose it is. It's from my managing clerk. He says: 'Something requiring your instant attention. Fear bad—' No—no—no reason in the world to suppose that D'yell has anything to do with it. I must just hurry away. I'm called upon often, you know," he added with a sickly explanatory smile, "on urgent—personal affairs."

"Oh yes," said Mrs. Dalyell, "we know that well; and no better or kinder counsellor. But you have had no breakfast—"

"I must not stop a moment longer—there is just time for the early train."

The girls caught their hats from the stand in the hall and ran down with him, Alice speeding on in front like a greyhound to bid the station-master keep back the train for a minute—a kindly arrangement which often was made for the convenience of Yalton. Mr. Wedderburn gave forth a few breathless instructions to Susie as he hurried along. "If I were you I would send over for Fred. He should be at home in the circumstances: and don't let your mother be troubled."

"But, dear Mr. Wedderburn, what are the circumstances?" said Susie. "Is there anything wrong with papa?"

"I hope not, my dear, I hope not. I've no reason to think that there is anything wrong: but just—I would have Fred at home as early as possible. And if I hear anything in town, I'll send you word directly. And you may calculate on seeing me before dinner. Then we'll know what to think."

"I hope papa will be home before then: and he'll laugh at us cardiatically."

"Susie, my dear—there's no such word."

"Oh yes, Mr. Wedderburn, for cardiac means from the heart; and that's the only way it will go."

He turned round upon her, and smiled with the strangest mixture of fatherly kindness and pity and sorrow. Susie was silenced by this strange look. Her eyes were startled with a sudden anxious question, her soft lips dropped apart with fear and wonder. "Oh, why are you so sorry for me, Mr. Wedderburn?" she cried. But they were just arriving at the railway, and the train was waiting. Susie, with her young sister clinging to her arm, both a little breathless with their run, in their light morning dresses and careless garden hats, the rose of morning health and brightness in their soft, shaded faces, the morning sun shining upon them and round them, distinguishing them upon the rustic platform by the soft little shadow they threw, was a sight the good lawyer never forgot. "The innocent things!" he said to himself.

When he was safe from their eyes, whirling along over the country, he took once more the telegram from his pocket: "Something requiring your immediate attention. Fear bad news. Sent for last night. Too late to communicate, please lose no time." Well! after all, there was nothing in that to indicate Bob D'yell. It might be Mrs. Davidson's business. It might be that scapegrace young Faulkner again. The devil fly away with all young spendthrifts! To give an honest man a fright like this for him! Mr. Wedderburn, with a momentary relief, noted, a gleam of fun coming into his eyes, two superfluous words in the telegram: "'Please'—the blockhead! What man in his senses says 'please' when he has to pay a ha'penny for it?" he said with a little hoarse laugh to himself. For surely it must be young Faulkner—the born fool! There was absolutely nothing to connect it with Bob D'yell.

When he entered his office, however, he was met with a very grave face by his managing clerk. "It was a man from Musselburgh, sir, last night. He came to the office, and finding it shut, as it naturally would be at that hour, came on to me at my house. You know, sir, I live out at Morningside—"

"It would be strange if I did not know where you live—get on, man, get on!"

"I say that to account for it being so late. Well, sir, he told me—if it was Musselburgh or if it was Portobello, I can't quite say, but it's written down, and I sent off young Gibson by skreigh of day to make inquiries. He told me, sir, that a heap of clothes had been found on the sands belonging to somebody, it would seem, that was bathing in the sea. They lay there all the afternoon and no one took any notice, but at last one of the fisherwomen getting bait came in and said it was a gentleman's clothes, and his watch and all lying. And the things were examined, and in the pockets were a number of letters—"

Mr. Wedderburn gave a gasp, inarticulate but impatient, with a vehement wave of his hand. The clerk handed him, with a look of deep commiseration and sympathy which filled the lawyer with sudden rage, a little packet on the table.

Ah!—had he not known it all the time?

He sank into a chair, speechless for the moment, but half with rage at Martin standing there gently shaking his head, with the look that a sympathetic acquaintance wears at a funeral—as if it were anything to him! "Robert Dalyell, Esq., Yalton," the familiar commonplace address, that meant nothing except the merest everyday necessity—that meant a whole tragedy now.

"Found lying on the sands. But was that all—was that all? For God's sake, man, speak out, whatever you have to say."

Martin excused Mr. Wedderburn's hastiness with a slight wave of his hand, and said all there was to say. It was very little: Mr. Dalyell, a man very well known, had been seen to arrive at the station, and had been met by various people on his way to the sea. He was not in the habit of using the bathing machines, as indeed few gentlemen were. There was no special danger about the spot, and it was a calm day, and he was a good swimmer. Of course the place was a little out of the way, and east of the sands, as was indispensable when gentlemen bathed without any machine; but nothing out of the ordinary—many men did the same, and Mr. Dalyell did it constantly. No cry of distress had been heard, nor any other signs of a catastrophe. This little mound of clothes, flung down with the conviction of perfect security, the watch in the pocket, a shilling or two dropped on the sands as the things were moved—this was all. "The body," Martin said, dropping his already subdued voice, "had not been found."

The body! Surely it was premature still to talk of that.

"He might have been carried along by the current further east and got to land there."

"A naked man, sir—without any clothes! There would soon have been word of such a wonder as that—and somebody sent on for the things. We took all that into consideration."

"I must go down myself at once," said the lawyer.

"I sent Gibson, sir, the first thing."

"What's Gibson to me?" said Mr. Wedderburn, with a sort of roar of trouble, anger, and misery combined. "I must go myself."

"There are a number of letters," said Martin, "that might want answering."

"Letters! when Bob Dalyell's lying somewhere dead or dying."

"Oh, sir," said Martin, "in the midst of life we are in death. If it's poor Mr. D'yell—and there's no reasonable doubt on the subject—he's dead long, long before now."

Wedderburn made a dash through the air with his clenched fist, as if he had been knocking down a too sympathetic clerk, and took his hat, and darted away.

"Old Pat's in one of his grandest tempers," a young clerk permitted himself to say in Mr. Martin's hearing, as the door closed with a violent swing behind their employer.

"Old Pat!—if it's our respected superior, Mr. Wedderburn, that ye mean by that familiar no to say contemptuous epithet," said Mr. Martin—"he has just heard of the loss of his dearest friend. You would do better to feel for him than to mock at a good man in trouble, my young friend."

Mr. Wedderburn rushed to Portobello as fast as the train would take him, following in the track of his young clerk, who had already exhausted every means of information, but who fortunately met the lawyer on the way and gave him the result of his inquiries. These inquiries seemed to leave no doubt as to the catastrophe, and Wedderburn found to his horror that it was already very generally known, and that there had been a paragraph on the subject in the Scotsman, fortunately not giving the name of the sufferer, but indicating the general fear that a well-known member of society had been the victim. "They never read the papers," Mr. Wedderburn said to himself, "and she would never think it was—him" (already it seemed too familiar to say Bob). When some one came hurrying up to him, grasping his hand and asking, "Is this awful news true?—is it out of doubt that it's poor D'yell?"—the broken-hearted man felt once more fiercely angry at the question, as if it was not a thing to be discussed in ordinary words. But this was morbid, he knew. The questioner was Mr. Scrymgeour, Fred's host, the giver of the ball on the previous night, who explained that he had seen the paragraph in the papers, and had secured it at once and come in to Edinburgh to inquire, that the poor boy should hear nothing till he could ascertain if it were true. And even while he spoke, others came pressing upon them with grave faces: "Was it true? Could it be D'yell?" The sensation was extraordinary. "He was said to be a little shaky in business matters," said one. "That was all rubbish," said another. "A man with a good estate at his back and plenty of friends—no fear but he would have pulled through." "And Chili stock is looking up again, which was supposed to be his danger." Thus they stood and talked him over. "I suppose there is no doubt it was an accident?" said another cautiously. This remark caught the lawyer's anxious ear, upon whose own heart a heavy cloud of dread was hanging. But there was a chorus (thank God!) of assurances. No, no!—Bob D'yell was the best fellow in the world. He was a man always confident in his own mind, a man that had every inducement to live—with a fine family, his son at Oxford, with a good estate behind him, and an excellent character and plenty of friends. Even if there might be a little temporary embarrassment—that would soon have blown over. There were men that would have stuck by him through thick and thin. "Me, for instance," said Mr. Wedderburn, careless of grammar. "I went out especially last night to tell him, if there really was trouble, I would see him through it—" "Poor fellow! Poor Bob! Poor D'yell!" the bystanders said in their various tones. Nobody had the faintest hope that he could have escaped. Such a prodigy as a man without clothes would soon have been known along the coast. And of course he would have hurried back, if he had been saved, to ease the anxieties of his friends. It was only Mr. Wedderburn who insisted upon every means being taken to secure the poor remains, and that not for certainty of the fact, but for decent burial. There is no coroner's inquest in Scotland; but an inquiry into all the circumstances was immediately set on foot, an inquiry at first in which there was no certain evidence but the piteous heap of clothes, the respectable garments in which every man of business goes to town. The papers left in the pocket, the few shillings on the sands, the notes in his pocket-book, were all so many unconscious witnesses to the accident, all proving how accidental, how unlooked-for, was this cutting short of his career. There was even a withered rose in his coat, a pale China rose from one corner of the terrace at Yalton, which Mr. Wedderburn recognised with a pang, as if it had been one of the children. The tears blinded the middle-aged lawyer's eyes as he took this faded thing out of his friend's coat, brushed off the sand from the withered leaves, and put it in his pocket-book reverently. All who were present looked on at this little incident as if it had been a religious rite.

It may be added here that the naked remains of a drowned man were found a few weeks afterwards on the east sands of Portobello. Needless to say that they were quite unrecognisable; but the height and size, and the absence of clothing, made it as nearly certain as any such thing could be that this was all that remained of Robert Dalyell.

Meanwhile that fatal day passed over at Yalton, the first part very quietly, as usual, in the ordinary occupations of the household. It was a beautiful morning, full of comfort and good hope, and Mrs. Dalyell was busy in her house. It was the day for the overseeing and paying of the weekly bills, and there were various repairs necessary before the winter set in which she had to look after, and a great deal of linen—napery as she called it—had come in from the laundry, which it was essential to examine to see what wanted renewing and what it would be possible to darn and keep in use. Old Janet Macalister was famous for her darning. Old as she was, it was still, Mrs. Dalyell said, "a pleasure to see" her work. It was an ornament to the tablecloths rather than a blemish. Old Janet was in great activity, almost agitation. She appeared in the house, as she very rarely did, and talked so much in an excited way, that the servants thought her "fey." She went with Mrs. Dalyell to the housekeeper's room, uninvited, to examine the linen. "Dinna put that away. I can darn that fine," old Janet said to many articles over which her mistress shook her head. "Losh! what's the good o' me, eatin' bread and burnin' fire this mony mony a year, if I canna keep the napery in order!" she cried. Her head, which was slightly palsied, nodded more than usual, her large pale hands shook; but her voice was strong, and she ended every sentence with a harsh laugh.

"I am afraid you are not very well to-day, Janet," said Mrs. Dalyell.

"Oh, 'deed am I, very well; but ye must give me work, mistress, ye must give me work. Without work there are o'er many thoughts in a person's head for comfort. And that fine darning, it just takes everything out of ye: it takes up baith body and mind."

When her survey of the linen was over, Mrs. Dalyell came back to the drawing-room, having sent old Janet back to her room with an armful of sheets and tablecloths. And she was glad to escape from the old woman. There was a gleam in her eyes, often fixed upon her mistress with a penetrating look, as if she knew something, and her unusual flurry of speech and the harsh laugh of agitation which occurred so often, which Mrs. Dalyell did not understand, and which alarmed her—she could not tell why. Then came luncheon, to which she sat down with her girls, with a forlorn sense of the two empty seats which Foggo had placed as usual. "I thought, mem," he said in his solemn way, "that Mr. Fred would have been home, if not the maister."

"Why should you think Mr. Fred would have been at home?" she asked almost angrily.

"He is coming in the afternoon with some of the young people from Westwood for tea. We shall want tea on the terrace at half-past four, and there will probably be five or six people."

"Very well, mem," said Foggo, more solemn than ever, and with a look which, like Janet's, meant more than his words.

Mrs. Dalyell had something like an attaque des nerfs, which was a malady unknown to her. She could not eat anything. In order that the servants might not suppose there was anything irregular in their master's proceedings, she said nothing before Foggo about her anxiety. She said she was tired, looking over all that weary linen. "And old Janet, that was stranger than ever, and she always was a strange creature. I think I will lie down for a little after lunch. And I almost wish that I had not bidden Fred to bring over the Scrymgeours with him for the afternoon." If this was said to throw dust in Foggo's eyes, Mrs. Dalyell might have spared herself the trouble. For Foggo had read his Scotsman that morning, and had heard a murmur of dismay which had come to Yalton by the backstairs, by the kitchen—nobody knew how. "God help the poor woman!" Foggo said, when he retired to his own domain, with more feeling than respect. "She's full of trouble, but she will not let on, and though she's in horror of something, it's not half so bad as what has come to pass."

"If that story's true," said the cook, who was too much disturbed and too anxious to hear everything to take any trouble about her own work, which the kitchen-maid was accomplishing sadly while her principal talked and cried over the dreadful rumour which had swept hither on the wings of the wind. "Oh, it's true enough," said Foggo, whose disposition was dismal—"and there's little dinner will be wanted here this night, for sooner or later they must hear. It was more than I could well bear to hear them talking of the big tea on the terrace and who was coming. I hope the Scrymgeour people will not be so mad as to let their young ones come: and nobody else will come, for it's well known over the country by this time, though she doesn't know."

"Oh, my poor bonnie lady," said the cook weeping—"and the kind maister, that had a pleasant word for everybody."

"Not so pleasant a word for them that crossed him," said Foggo. "Not that I would say a word against him, and him a drowned man."

Early in the afternoon Fred came home. It was a house that stood always with open doors and windows, so that there was no need to open to any familiar comer; but Foggo was in the hall, chiefly because he too was excited and eager to have the first of any news that might arrive, when the youth with his light step came in. His eager question, "Is my father at home?" made the grave butler more solemn than ever.

"No, sir, the master has not been back since he left the house yesterday morning," said Foggo.

But though his looks were so significant, that the very dogs saw that something was the matter, Fred neither gave nor communicated any news. He rushed upstairs three steps at a time, and burst into the drawing-room, where his mother was sitting. She had tried to lie down, as she had said, but Mrs. Dalyell could not rest: her nerves would not be stilled, and her thoughts grew so many that they buzzed in her ears, and seemed to suffocate her in her throat. She was sitting at the window which commanded the gate, so that she might see who appeared, ever watching for that telegraph boy, who in a moment might set all right.

"You have come back early, Fred," she said. "And have you come alone?"

"Mother, what's this I hear, that my father has never come home?"

"Who has told you such a thing? Your father has many affairs in his hands; he's often been called away in a hurry."

"You knew then he was going somewhere? It's all right, then, thank God!" said Fred; "and that dreadful thing in the papers has nothing to do with him."

"What dreadful thing in the papers?" cried Mrs. Dalyell. It was not till Fred had thus committed himself in his haste and anxiety that he felt how foolish it was to refer to a report which as yet was not authenticated. He went to look for the papers, cursing his own rashness. But Foggo had more sense than might have been supposed. He had conveyed that Scotsman out of the way.

Alas! as if it were of any use to try to stave off the knowledge of such a calamity! An hour later Mr. Wedderburn's sober step sounded upon the gravel, coming up from the train. Mrs. Dalyell sat still in her chair, not running to meet him as the others did. "Oh, I shall hear it soon enough—I shall hear it soon enough!" she said to herself.

His very step had tragedy in it; and she knew before she saw him that something dreadful had happened, that the failure of that telegram, which Robert had never before omitted to send her, was but too well explained. Something like a sweeping gust of fatal wind seemed to flow through the house—a chill consciousness of coming trouble, calling out everybody from above and below to hear the news. And then there was a terrible cry, and then a dread stillness fell over Yalton—like the stillness before a storm.

There was one strange thing, however, which happened that fatal afternoon, and which Fred could never forget. As he went upstairs to his own room, which was in the upper storey, a pale and miserable ghost of the cheerful youth he had been yesterday, he saw old Janet standing at the end of the passage which led to her room. She put out her long arm, out of the folds of her tartan shawl. "How is she taking it, Mr. Fred?" she asked. Janet's eyes were deep, and shone with a strange fire. Her face was full of excitement and agitation—but not of grief, although she had been devoted to the master, who was also her nursling. "How is your mother taking it?" There was a gleam of strange curiosity in her eyes.

"Taking it?" cried Fred. "Have you no heart that you ask such a question? My mother is heartbroken—as we all are," said the lad, his voice giving way to the half-arrested sob, which he was too young to be able to restrain.

"But no me—that's what you're thinking: though the Lord knows he's more to me than everything else in this world. Laddie, you're young—young; and so is your mother. But me, I'm a very old woman. I've seen many a strange thing. You'll mind that you're to come and ask me if you're ever very sore troubled in your mind."

"You!" cried Fred. There was something like scorn in his tone. The first distress of youth seems always final, insurmountable, so that it is half an insult to suggest that it will be lived through and other troubles come. But then a sudden chill of horror came over the lad. "You!" he said again, with a pang which he did not himself understand. He remembered what his father had said: "Go to old Janet." Did she know what his father had said? Had she been aware that this great trouble, this more than trouble, this misery, calamity, was coming? Fred gave the old woman an awed and terrified look—and fled: from her and his own thoughts.

CHAPTER V

There is no coroner's inquest in Scotland, as has been said; nevertheless there was a careful examination into all the circumstances of Mr. Dalyell's death. It was known that he was going to Portobello to bathe. This he had stated not only to his family, but to the clerks at the insurance office and other persons whom he had met. One gentleman appeared who had travelled that little journey with him by the train, whom he had almost persuaded to join him in his swim, and who parted with him only at the corner of the road leading down to the sands; the porter at the station had seen him arrive, had seen the two walk off together. There was no mystery or concealment about anything he had done. It was his usual place for bathing, there was nothing extraordinary about the matter, up to the moment when the clothes were found on the sands and the man was gone. Every step was traced of his ordinary career, nor could one suspicious circumstance be found. The mere fact of the heap of clothing, the money in the pockets, the watch, all the familiar careless evidences of a day which was to be as any other day, with no auguries of evil in it, was all there was to account for his disappearance. But that was pathetically distinct and unimpeachable. And when after so much delay the body was found—which, indeed, no one could tell to be Robert Dalyell's body, but which by every law of probability might be considered so—the question dropped, and all the endless talk and speculation to which it had given rise. Of course there were doubts at first whether it might be suicide. But why, of all people in the world, should Robert Dalyell drown himself? No doubt there had been rumours of unfortunate speculations, and possible pecuniary disaster. But everybody knew now that Pat Wedderburn, a man of considerable wealth and unlimited credit, had put his means at his friend's disposal. It is true that what Mr. Wedderburn had said was that he was about to do so; but these fine shades are too much to be preserved when a statement is sent about from mouth to mouth, and all Edinburgh was persuaded that Mr. Wedderburn's means made Dalyell's position secure—if, indeed, it ever was insecure, with a good estate behind him, and all his connections. But what a fatality! What a catastrophe! A man in the prime of life, with a nice wife and delightful children, a charming place, an excellent position, everything smiling upon him. That he should be carried away from all that in a moment by some confounded cramp, some momentary weakness. What a lesson it was! In the midst of life we are in death. This was what, with many regrets for Bob D'yell and sorrow for his family, and a great sensation among all who knew him, Edinburgh said. And then the event was displaced by another event, and his name was transferred from the papers and everybody's mouth to a tablet in Yalton Church, and Robert Dalyell was as if he had never been.

It proved that his life was very heavily insured—to a much larger sum than anybody had been aware of, and in several offices. Neither Mrs. Dalyell, nor any of his advisers knew the reason for these unusual liberalities of arrangement, if not that Mr. Dalyell, being himself concerned in an insurance office, thought it right to set an example to others by the number and value of his own. Enough was obtained in this sorrowful way to clear off everything that was wrong in his affairs, and to secure Fred, when he should come of age, in unencumbered possession of Yalton, as well as to leave the portions of the girls intact. So far as this went, and though it was a dreadful thing to think, much more to say, no doubt it passed through Mr. Wedderburn's mind, who was the sole executor, with the exception of Mrs. Dalyell, that the moment of poor Bob's death was singularly well chosen. Mrs. Dalyell left everything in his hands, so that the conclusion was in no way forced upon her, nor would she have entertained it if it had occurred to her. Nothing would have persuaded her that her Robert had drowned himself, and she knew no reason why. She was not a woman who demanded explanations, who searched into the motives of things. She accepted the event when it happened with sorrow or with thankfulness, according as it was good or bad, but she did not demand to have the secret told her of how it came about. And she grieved deeply for her good husband; the earth was altogether overcast to her for a time. She felt no warmth in the sun, no beauty in the world—a pall hung over everything. Robert was gone—what was the good of all those secondary things, the comforts and ease of life, which were not him, nor ever could bring him back? She would have accepted joyfully a life of poverty and privation with Robert instead of this dreadful comfortable blank without him. Her emotions were as sincere as they were sober and unexaggerated. But, as was natural, this gloom of early bereavement did not last. After a few months she was capable of taking a little pleasure in the spring weather, of watching the flowers come up. And though the first notice she took of these ameliorating circumstances was to say with tears, "How pleased your father always was to see the crocuses!" yet it was the beginning of a better time. Mrs. Dalyell was still in the forties; she was in excellent health, and she was of a mild, unimpassioned temperament. It was not possible that the clouds should hang for ever about such a tranquil sky.

But there were two of the mourners who were not so simply constituted. Fred, who had been so light-hearted a boy when his father talked to him on the terrace and bade him think of the catastrophes which overturned so many young lives, was greatly changed. He could not get that conversation out of his mind, nor the strange recommendation his father had given him, nor the stranger repetition by old Janet of what Mr. Dalyell had said. How did she know? Had the father confided to her what was about to happen? Confided?—a thing which was an accident, an unforeseen calamity, or—— what else? Confided to Janet that next day he was going to die? Fred turned this over in his mind, over and over, till he was nearly mad. How did she know? How did she know? Was it second-sight, witchcraft of one kind or another? But Fred was a young man of his time—or rather he was not sufficiently a young man of his time to believe in witchcraft or any occult power. How was it?—how was it?—how was it? This question went on in his mind so constantly that it became a sort of mechanical rhyme running through everything. How did old Janet know? Had it been discovered by her somehow by mystic art? Had it been confided to her? He could not turn his mind away from this question or forget it. How did she know?—what did she know? Fred felt as if he should have informed the commissioners who had investigated the circumstances of his father's death of that conversation on the terrace. It might be only a coincidence; but it was a very curious coincidence. He ought to have reported it, made it known, that everybody might draw his own conclusions. Here was a man who as a matter of fact died by some mysterious accident next day, and who had talked to his son of what he might have to do were he left with the family on his hands, and advised whom he should take counsel with in difficulties: and the proposed counsellor had apparently been communicated with too. What would the little court of inquiry, he wondered, have said to that? What would the insurance people have said? Was it his duty to have told the strange and terrible detail? Was it better to have remained silent? Poor Fred could not tell what he ought to have done—what he ought to do. He was but a boy after all, when all was said. He had not been accustomed to form such momentous decisions for himself, and he was overwhelmed with grief and misery, not able to think. He remained silent, not betraying even to Mr. Wedderburn, who was now the guide of the household, looking after everything, what he felt. But the lad was very unhappy. There was no reason why he should not return to Oxford; but he had no desire to return. He did not care to do anything. He wandered about the grounds asking himself what his father meant, if he had it all in his mind then as he walked along the terrace in the dark, listening to his boy's chatter of college jokes and light-hearted nonsense. Was he thinking then of what was to be done next day? Had he planned it all? and left perhaps his last instructions with Janet, the unlikeliest repository of such secrets. Could it be this? or only coincidence, a series of coincidences, such as may occur and sometimes do occur, perplexing and confusing every calculation? All this made him very miserable, as he pondered, many a weary monotonous night and day. He stole out in the evenings after dinner and strolled along the terrace, as his father had been used to do, with a sort of vague hope of enlightenment, of some influence that might come to him, or even voice that he might hear. But he never heard anything more than the wind moaning in the trees, which drove him indoors with the melancholy of their unseen rustling, and the eerie sounds of the night, rising over all the invisible country, tinkle of water, and sweeping sound of the winds and the drop of the autumnal leaves falling, the hoot of an owl, the stirring of unseen things in the woods and fields. But when he was indoors again, still less could Fred bear the cheerful air of the drawing-room with its bright fire and lamps, and the voices of his sisters which began after a time of silence to whisper and chatter again in the irrepressible vitality of their youth. Had it all been planned before that night? Did his father already well know what was going to happen on the morrow—all the incidents of the tragedy? And did Janet know? Fred repeated these questions to himself till his brain felt as if it were giving way.

All this time he kept himself carefully away from speech or look of Janet, who had been, strange as it was, less affected by the calamity than any one in the house, and had a look in her dry eyes which Fred could not understand. His heart revolted against her; a woman without feeling, who had no tears for the man who had surrounded her with comforts and ensured her well-being for her life—the man who was her child, whom she had nursed, but never mourned. A sort of hatred sprang up in the lad's mind towards this old woman. He felt it a wrong and almost insult that he should have been bidden to take her advice—and avoided her as if she had been the plague. Janet, on the contrary, seemed to seek opportunities of encountering him, appearing suddenly about the house, as she had never hitherto done, in all kinds of unlikely places. Her unobtrusiveness had been one of her great qualities in former times. She had never been seen on the stairs or in the corridor, scarcely at all, except at the opening of the passage leading to her own room, or sitting in the sun by the laundry door, or about the servants' part of the house. But now old Janet seemed to be everywhere. Fred met her in the hall, lingering about the library, in the gallery above which encircled the hall, everywhere save in his mother's drawing-room. And whenever she met him, though she did nothing to stop him, she gave him a look full of significance. It seemed to say, "When are you coming to consult me? I want to be consulted," till the young man became exasperated, and fled from her with an ever-growing sense of trouble or fear. Her apparition in her large white mutch, with a black ribbon round it, tied in a great bow on the top of her head, with her black and white shepherd's plaid shawl, which she had adopted, instead of the old red and green tartan, in compliment to the family mourning—gave him a sensation of shivering, as if old Janet had included in her own person the properties of all the Fates. He was afraid of what she might have to say to him— afraid lest there should be something to tell which would be hateful to hear; afraid for his father's good name and his own peace.

Mr. Wedderburn had no such addition to the many cares which this catastrophe had introduced into his placid life. He knew nothing about Janet, or any secret she might have in her keeping, nor had he any idea of that last interview which lay so heavily upon Fred's mind; but he was not at ease. The public mind had been entirely reassured on the subject of Dalyell's embarrassed circumstances by the announcement that Pat Wedderburn had taken upon him all the responsibility and was indeed the principal in Dalyell's speculations, using him only as an agent, which was what Wedderburn's statement on the subject had now grown to. But Wedderburn knew very well that he had only intended to make this offer to his friend, and that Dalyell's troubles about money were weighing very heavily upon him when he went down to Portobello for his swim. And he knew that the very opportune cramp or failure of heart which caused his death accomplished at the same time the complete deliverance from all those cares, of his children and his wife. Everything was appropriate, perfectly convenient to the moment and to the needs of the man who gave his life for his family as much as if he had defended them to the death on the ramparts of some besieged city—with this only exception, that the weapons with which he fought were equivocal, if not dishonest. For the insurance money would never have been paid to the representatives of a suicide. Poor Bob! poor Bob! it was unworthy, it was dreadful to associate that title with his honest name. And yet—if it had been a planned thing, it was not an honest thing, although he had paid for it by the sacrifice of his life. This thought rankled in Mr. Wedderburn's mind. Dalyell had been, so to speak, absolved by public opinion from that guilt. The payment of the insurances was in itself a full acquittal, and no one ventured to say or even think that the catastrophe on the Portobello sands was anything but a fatal accident. But Wedderburn's mind was haunted by this doubt. It was not for him to bring it forward, to hint a suspicion which could never be proved, which would be ruinous to the prospects of those whose interests were in his hands. No, never to any soul would he hint such a doubt. But yet—he said to himself that poor Bob would have been capable of it. A thing that you are willing to give your life to purchase—it is difficult to believe that what is bought at such a sacrifice could be wronging any one, or a sin against the commonwealth. The suicide would be a sin before God, but many a desperate creature is ready to encounter that, with a pathetic trust in the understanding and pity of the great Father. But to die dishonestly for the good of your family, that was a different thing. Bob Dalyell, perhaps, was not a man who would attach any idea of guilt to this way of cheating the insurance companies, even his own office; but Wedderburn, who might have been capable of the sacrifice, would have stood at that. His idea of honour and probity was perhaps more abstract than that of a man who was involved in sharp business transactions, in speculation and commercial adventure, and who was, besides, a man with a family, bent upon saving them from ruin. He shook his head and acknowledged to himself that poor Bob was capable of not having taken that divergence from strict integrity into account. Had he made up his mind to die for his family he would not have considered the ease of the insurance companies. The thought of wronging them would have sat lightly on his soul.

Mr. Wedderburn took from this self-discussion a habit which remained with him for all the rest of his life, the habit of shaking his head, slowly, sadly to himself, as it were, as if in the course of some remark. It was while he questioned, and doubted, and laid things together, excusing his friend even while he judged him, that this habit was acquired. It was not a bad habit for a lawyer who was consulted by his clients on many delicate questions. It gave an air of regretful decision, of compassion and sympathy, when he had conclusions to announce that were not pleasant to his clients. And he never lost this gesture of reflection and compassion, which was as sacred to Bob Dalyell as his tombstone. It was thus, with many a vexing doubt and fear, that he mourned the friend of his youth.

The female members of the party were happily exempted from all these discussions. It does not often happen that the women have the lightest part to bear in any such calamity. But in this case it was so. Mrs. Dalyell mourned her husband most sincerely and deeply, forgetting every little flaw in his character, and gradually elevating him into the position of a perfect man—the best husband, the kindest father! And the girls mourned him with torrents of youthful tears, with a conviction that they never could smile again, never get beyond the blackness of the first grief, the awful sensation of the catastrophe. But there was nothing but pure sorrow in their minds. They thought no more of the insurance companies than the birds in the garden think of the crumbs miraculously provided for them when snow is on the ground. Neither had the slightest doubt ever entered their minds as to what they were told of his death. They knew every detail, laying it up in their hearts. How he had parted smiling from his friend at the corner of the street, and gone off to the sands with his buoyant step, in such health and strength, in such good-will and good-humour with all the world. This was what the girls said to themselves, trying to picture his last look upon life. And they hoped it was some unsuspected failure of the heart, which the doctor said was most likely—a thing which would give no pain, which would be over in a moment, so that he would never know he was dying, or have any pang of anxiety for those he was leaving behind. This was how the girls realised their father's death: and their mother's picture of it was not dissimilar. She felt that there must have been a moment in which he thought of her and of "the bairns." Mrs. Dalyell added that to the imaginary scene—a moment in which, as people said was the case in drowning, all his life would rush through his brain, and he would think of her as he died. They had the best of it. Their innocent thoughts conceived no ulterior scheme, no darkness of doubt. Had they realised that any such doubt existed, it is probable that they would have canonised poor Robert Dalyell on the spot as a hero and martyr, dying for those he loved, and still never have thought of the insurance companies; but, happily, no such imagination entered at all into their simple thoughts.

The household had settled down completely into the habits of its new life, when Fred Dalyell came home from a long wandering tour he had made about Europe, not so much for love of travelling or desire to see beautiful things and places, as to distract his mind from the miserable thoughts that had gained so complete an empire over him. He had succeeded very well in that, for the most persistent trouble yields to such treatment at twenty; but the first return to Yalton, and all the recollections that were waiting for him under those familiar trees, brought back on the first coming much of the old trouble to the lad's sensitive mind. It was now May, and Yalton was almost as cheerful as ever, though in a subdued way. The girls, "poor things," as their mother said, had recovered their spirits. They were so young!—and Fred's coming home had been a thing much looked for, like the beginning of a new era to the young creatures over whom the winter of gloom was naturally passing away. Susie and Alice were much disappointed by the cloud that came over Fred after the first joy of their greetings. Instead of sitting with them and telling them everything, he disappeared on the first evening, with a sort of impatient, almost angry, resistance of their blandishments.

"Oh, let me alone; I have a thousand things to think of," he said, pushing them away as the manner of big brothers is. Susie and Alice forgave Fred when they saw the little red tip of his cigar on the terrace, and realised that he had gone there "to think of father." For a moment it was debated between them whether one of them should not go to him to share his solitude and thoughts; but they decided, with a better inspiration, to leave him alone, and even withdrew delicately from the drawing-room window, not to seem to spy upon his sacred thoughts.

"Oh, do you mind how papa used to go up and down, up and down?" said Alice to Susie.

"Do I mind?" said Susie, half indignant. "Could I ever forget?" And they shed a few tears together, then hurried off to the table in the full light of the lamps, where Fred's curiosities which he had brought home, and all his little presents, were laid out for inspection, and began to laugh and twitter over them, and compare this with that, like two birds.

Yes, this was just the place where father had stood when he had suddenly changed the conversation about the bump-suppers, and all the joys of Oxford, to that strange and sober talk about the vicissitudes of life, and what a difference a day might make in the position of a happy lad at college, thinking of nothing but fun and frolic. Fred remembered every word, every look—the wail of the autumnal wind, the clear break of sky among the clouds towards the west, the half shock, half amusement, with which he had felt that sudden change into what in those days of levity he had called the didactic in his father's tone. It had seemed to him a sermon at the time; and then it had seemed to him—he knew not what— an awful advertisement of what was coming: a prophecy conscious or unconscious. He walked up and down, up and down under the trees, hearing the same sounds, the tinkle of the half-choked fountain, the rustling of the wind among the branches. The sentiment of the night was different, for that had been in September, and this was full of the soft and hopeful stir of May. The leaves were falling then; now they were but just opened, hanging in clusters of vivid young green, which almost forced colour upon the paleness of the wistful night. But nothing else was as it had been then. His father was gone, swept from the earth as though he had never been. Yet this great change had not brought the other changes which Mr. Dalyell anticipated. Fred had not been forced into the premature development of a young head of the family. He had not been plunged into care and trouble, into work and anxiety. If anything, he had been more free than before. He was still only a youth dallying upon the edge of life, not a man entering into serious duties. The contrast struck him strangely. This was not what his father had foreseen. It gave him a vague new trouble in his mind to perceive that this was so. He ought to be less free, perhaps more occupied, more responsible. He could not all at once decide what the difference was.

Here he was suddenly disturbed by the sound of a step upon the gravel—and it is to be feared that Fred uttered within himself an impatient exclamation, as he threw away the end of his cigar. "Here is one of those bothering girls," he said to himself, though we know with what high reason and feeling Susie and Alice had withdrawn, even from the window, not to seem to spy upon their brother. He got up to meet them, remembering that he had just come home and that it would be brutal to show any impatience of their affection. But Fred might have known that the heavy, slow step which approached him was not that of either of the girls. A tall figure shaped itself out of the darkness—the white mutch, the bow of black ribbon, the checked shawl, became dimly visible.

"Eh, Mr. Fred," said old Janet, "but I'm blythe to see you home!"

"Oh," he said, "it's you!" in a tone which was not encouraging. He had forgotten old Janet, happily, and it was with anything but pleasure that he felt her image thus thrust upon him again.

"Who should it be but me?" she said. "There is none that can take such an interest. And, Mr. Fred, it is time you should be taking your ain place. This house of Yalton should go into no other hands but them it belongs to. Oh, I canna speak more plain; but you must rouse yourself up, and you must take your ain place."

"I don't know what you have to do with it," cried Fred angrily, "nor why you should thrust your advice upon me. I am here in my own place. What do you mean? I ought to be at Oxford, that would be my own place."

"Na, na! that would be just more schooling," said Janet, "and it's no schooling you want, but to stand up like a man, and be maister of your father's house, as is your right. Oh, laddie, I tell you I canna speak more plain; but take you my word, it'll save more trouble, and worse trouble, if you will just grip the reins in your hands and take your ain place!"

He laughed contemptuously in his impatience and anger. "You had better save your advice for things you understand," he said. "Don't you know the law considers me an infant, and that I can do nothing till I'm of age—if there was anything to do? But all is going as well as can be—almost too well—as if he were not missed," the young man cried abruptly with a movement of feeling, which indeed was momentary and had not come into his mind before. Perhaps it was an influence from the brain of the old woman beside him which sent it there now.

"That's just what I wanted to say," said old Janet—"as if he were not missed. All settled for her, and smoothed down and made fair and easy, as if himsel' were to the fore. There's trouble in the air, Mr. Fred, and if you dinna bestir yourself, and take your ain place, and get a grip of the reins in your ain hand—"

"Rubbish!" said Fred. "How can I get the reins, till I come of age? If there was any need, which there is not, my mother knows better than half a dozen of me."

"Your mother!" said old Janet, with the natural contempt of an old servant for the mistress; then she added in a different tone: "if it was only your mother"—shaking her old head.

"Who else?" said Fred with indignation. But Janet made no reply. She turned her back upon him and went off along the terrace, always shaking her head, which was slightly palsied and had a faint nodding motion besides. Something in this confirmed movement which was comic, and the jealousy of his mother, which had always been a well-known feature in old Janet, tended to give a ludicrous character to her appeal. Instead of deepening the sadness of his thoughts, it lightened them with a curious sense of relief. It seemed to take away at once the gravity of the recollection of his father's reference to her, and the painful suggestion in it which had caused Fred so much trouble, when old Janet thus displayed herself in an absurd rather than a tragical light.

CHAPTER VI

Mr. Wedderburn entered very naturally into the charge of his friend's affairs. He had been Dalyell's counsellor already on many occasions in his life, and knew much about his concerns, the resources of the estate, and all the original sources of income which Dalyell had increased, yet fatally risked, by his speculations. No one was better fitted than he to apply the welcome aid of the insurance moneys to the relief of Yalton from all the encumbrances which the dead man's other affairs had imported into his life. A man so familiar with the household and all its affairs, nobody could know so well as he how to guide the revenues of the household so as to afford their usual comforts to Mrs. Dalyell and the girls without injuring Fred's interests, or forgetting the very near approach of the time when he should take the control into his own hands. It was evident that changes were inevitable then; either that Mrs. Dalyell should retire to a house of her own, or that she should remain as Fred's housekeeper, with her authority contingent upon his plans, and liable to be destroyed whenever the young man should think of marriage—a position in which the faithful friend of the house was unwilling to contemplate the mistress of Yalton. It was not a thing that would have affected Mrs. Dalyell. It would not have occurred to her to think that the house was less hers by being Fred's. But Mr. Wedderburn was jealous of her dignity, and it wounded a certain imaginative sense of fitness for which no one would have given the dry old lawyer credit—the notion that the woman whom he had so long admired and liked should be dependent on her boy's caprice and whether it should please him or not to marry. The event which would make another change, so great, in her position, troubled him more than he could say. Was it not enough, he asked himself, that she should have had this shock to bear, and her life rent in two, that she should now have to yield all authority to Fred, and be dependent upon him for her home and dignity? The thought did not disturb Mrs. Dalyell, who felt it as natural to continue as before at the head of a house, which was no less hers because her son was now its formal head, as to perform any other act of life. But it did disturb her champion and guardian, who made it more and more his office from day to day to watch over her comfort and spare her trouble.

It was astonishing how Pat Wedderburn, who had not for many years, indeed for all his independent life, known more of the sweets of domesticity than those which he shared at second-hand in the houses of his friends, and especially at Yalton, fell into the ways of the head of a family. He did not, indeed, come out to Yalton every night as poor Dalyell had done, but he spent at least half of his evenings there, and gave his mind to the consideration of what was wanted in the house, and what would be agreeable to both mother and girls, with a curious familiar devotion which was at once amusing and touching. No father probably ever was so mindful of the tastes of his children as Mr. Wedderburn was of Susie and Alice. He remembered what they liked, and noted every expression of a wish with an affectionate vigilance and thoughtfulness which surprised even the girls, though they were well accustomed to have their little caprices considered. As for Mrs. Dalyell, no wife ever had her likings more sedulously consulted, her suggestions more carefully carried out, than were hers by her co-executor, her trustee, and fellow-guardian of the children. She had but to speak to Mr. Wedderburn about any trifling obstacle and it was immediately removed out of their way. He regarded her wants and wishes as things which were sacred; not as a husband does, whose natural impulse it is to contest, if not to deny. Life had never been made so easy for the ladies of Yalton. When he came out it was almost certain that some pleasant surprise accompanied him—a book, a present, something that either girls or mother had wished for. And they all took Mr. Wedderburn as completely for granted as if this devotion had been the most natural thing in the world.

And it would be impossible to describe the sweetness that came into the life of old Pat Wedderburn (as Edinburgh profanely called him) from this amateur performance, so to speak, of the duties of husband and father. He had long been in the habit of considering Yalton as a sort of home. But yet his visits there, though he was always so welcome, were more or less at the pleasure of his hosts, and he had kept up the form, though it was not much more than a form, of being invited. Now no such restraint (though it had never been much of a restraint) existed. He put a certain limit upon himself, but save for that the house of his wards was to him as his own, always open, always ready. They were all his wards, the mother not less than the children. It is true she was joined with him in the trust, and that she was a woman, as he said to himself, of a great deal of sense, who could give him advice upon many subjects, and even took or appeared to take an intelligent interest in investments, and knew whether the claims of the farmers were just, and what was right in respect to repairs, &c., better than Mr. Wedderburn himself. But she had never been accustomed to do anything for herself, to act independently, to take any step without advice and active help. It is impossible to say how pleasant it was to the middle-aged bachelor to be thus referred to at every moment asked about everything, consulted in every domestic contingency. He would not have minded even had he been called upon to settle difficulties with the servants, or subdue a refractory cook, nor would it have bored him to have a housekeeper's afflictions in this way poured into his ears.

Happily, however, in the large easy-going household at Yalton there were few difficulties of that kind. Mrs. Dalyell was an excellent manager, but she was not exacting, and her servants were chiefly old servants, who ruled the less permanent kitchen-maids, footboys, &c., under them with rods of iron, but did not trouble the mistress with their imperfections. When a house has been long established on such a footing, and there is no overwhelming necessity for economy, or interfering dispositions on the part of its head, it is wonderful how smoothly it will roll on, notwithstanding all human weaknesses. And the shadow of grief glided away. There could not have been a more desirable house, or a more pleasant routine of life. The very neighbourhood breathed peace into Wedderburn's being. Before he had reached the gates the atmosphere of content enveloped him. He had something in his pocket for the girls—he had something to consult their mother about, generally her own business, but sometimes even his, so great a confidence was he acquiring in her common-sense. To think that the loss of poor Bob Dalyell should have brought so great an acquisition of happiness into his life! He was ashamed when he came to think of it, and felt a compunction as if he had profited by his friend's disaster. But it was no fault of his.

And there was no doubt that Mr. Wedderburn enjoyed Yalton and the life there a great deal more than if he had been really the father whose office as far as possible he had taken upon himself. He was not responsible for the faults or aggrieved by the imperfections of the children, as a man is to whom they belong. The very distance between them increased the charm. Although it would have been death to him to have been thrust out of that paradise, it would perhaps have lessened its charm had he been absolutely swept into it, bound to it, by law and necessity. The freedom of the voluntary tie added sweetness to the bond. He was far more at the orders of his adopted family than any father would have been; but that shyness of old bachelorhood, which is as real as the reserve of old maidenhood and very similar, though it is little remarked, was in no way ruffled or wounded by the present arrangement. And thus good came out of all the evil, to one at least of the little circle who had been so deeply affected by it. Poor Bob D'yell!—to think that he should have lost all this, and that his most devoted friend should have acquired it by his loss! This gave Mr. Wedderburn a compunction which was of course entirely fictitious and visionary—for had he not taken that position it would have been much worse for the family as well as for himself.

This state of affairs was scarcely interrupted by Fred's majority, for Fred, no more than any other member of the household, considered that it made any difference. Of course, in the progress of time he would marry, and probably desire to be as his father had been. But, in the meantime, he felt himself no less a boy on the morning after his twenty-first birthday than he had done the morning before; and the idea of taking the reins out of his mother's hands or desiring more freedom than he actually possessed, especially the freedom of turning her out of the house which was now legally his, or disturbing any of her arrangements, never occurred to Fred. Young people brought up under such an easy sway as that of Mrs. Dalyell do not feel the temptation of rushing wildly into freedom as soon as it is legally their own. Fred had always been free, and he could not be more so, because his name was now at the head of all the family affairs, and Frederick Dalyell, Esq., was now the official proprietor at Yalton. What difference did it make? The family generally said none. Of course, Fred, as the only son and the eldest, would have been paramount in the house under any circumstances; he could not be more than paramount now. But it was not to Fred that Mrs. Dalyell looked for help and advice, any more than it had been before; this birthday did not add experience or wisdom to the boy. And Mr. Wedderburn came and went just the same, looking after Fred's interests, spoiling the girls, always ready to be referred to. It made no difference, nor did anybody wish that it should, except perhaps old Janet, whose opinion was not thought much of, whom Fred avoided carefully, and whose very existence was scarcely realised by the adviser of the house. As for Fred himself, his troubled thoughts had worn themselves out. Whatever trouble there may be in the mind respecting a man who has been in his grave for more than a year, it dies away under the progress of gentle time. To keep up the pressure of such misery there must be new events occurring or to be dreaded. What is altogether past affects the spirit in a different way. If there was a tragic secret unrevealed in the story of Robert Dalyell's death, it was hidden for ever in the bitter waves that had swallowed him up: and the course of his young life had gradually swept from Fred's mind the burden of his father's tragedy. He had decided to go back to Oxford at the end of the first year, and he was still continuing his unlaborious studies there when the second had ended, and October, with its shortening days and windy skies, returned again. The vacation had been a lively one to Fred, and Mrs. Dalyell had been obliged to come out of the seclusion of her widowhood on account of Susie, whose introduction to the world could not be postponed any longer. Mrs. Dalyell herself was not unwilling that it should be so. She was entirely contented in her home-life, yet pleased to vary it when need was, and the more smiling and brilliant side of things no longer jarred upon her feelings. And Susie, in all the fervour of her first season (though it was only in Edinburgh), was as happy as the day.

Thus it was, upon a household as cheerful as could be seen, that the shadows began to lengthen in that October, a little before the end of the vacation, when Fred, who had exhausted his own covers with the assistance of his friends, was flitting about the country in a series of "last days" before he went back to his college. Fred's friends of the shooting parties had made the house very gay for the girls, and Mr. Wedderburn had thought it expedient to "put in an appearance," as he said, even more frequently than usual, to support Mrs. Dalyell and help to preserve the balance of the house. He came "out" four or five nights in the week to the house which became daily more and more like his home, and found a continually increasing charm in the sight of the pleasure of the young ones and in the company of their mother. While they were carrying on their amusements, he considered it only his duty to sit by Mrs. Dalyell and keep her as far as possible from feeling the blank of the empty place. They could talk to each other, as only old friends can—of the people and places they had mutually known all their lives, of the different dispositions of the children, of Robert, how pleased he would have been to see them so happy, of the beasts in the little home-farm; and of the new leases, and the new Lord of Session, and the Queen's visit to Edinburgh, and everything indeed that came within the range of their kindly world. It was very pleasant: Mrs. Dalyell found it so, who was thus able to relieve her mind of any remark that occurred to her, which the young ones were too hasty or too much occupied to listen to; and Mr. Wedderburn liked it still better, feeling that he himself, who had never ventured to risk any of the great undertakings of life, had thus come to have the cream and perfection of quiet social comfort, without paying for it, without cost to himself or wrong to any one in life.

On one such evening Mrs. Dalyell had been called away on some domestic errand, and Mr. Wedderburn, feeling thus a little left to himself, strolled out upon the terrace to look at the rising moon and to enjoy the softness of the evening, one of the last perhaps before the winter came on. It was a still night, and the temperature was high for the time of year. The country had been blazing in the sunlight with all the colours of the autumn, and even the moon brought out the yellow lightness in the waving birches, if not the russet reds and browns of the deeper foliage. Nothing could be more still: the sky resplendent, with here and there a puff of ethereal whiteness, a cloud scarcely to be called a cloud, imperceptibly floating upon a breeze that was scarcely to be called a breeze—a soft sigh of night air. It was so warm that he did not hesitate to sit down, though at fifty-seven one is cautions about sitting down in the open-air in October, even in the day. But the night was very soft, and so were Mr. Wedderburn's thoughts. It cannot be said they were sentimental, much less impassioned. He wanted no more than he possessed, the loving kindness of this house, the affection of the children, the friendship and trust of their mother. He was entirely satisfied to come and go, to feel that he was of use to them, to enjoy their society. A great sense of well-being filled his mind as he sat there and heard the sound of their young voices gay and sweet coming from the billiard-room, where Fred and a friend or two were amusing the girls. There was something like a suggestion that more might come of that partnership of jest and play which was springing up between pretty Susie and one of these young men—dear little Susie!—who had given up her big words, but whom her father's friend still corrected and petted with fatherly tenderness. If it were possible to feel more fatherly than old Pat Wedderburn, the dry old Edinburgh lawyer, felt as he sat there and smiled in the dark at the sound of Susie's voice, I do not know what that quintessence of paternity could be.

He was thus sitting in quiet enjoyment of the solitude (which is so much sweeter a thing with the sense of the near vicinity of those we love than when we are really alone) and his own thoughts, when he saw, as Fred had done on a previous occasion, a tall figure rise as it were out of the soil and approach through the dark—a shadow, but with that independent movement of a living creature which is so instantly distinguishable from any combination of shadows. Mr. Wedderburn was not superstitious, but the figure as it came slowly towards him was one which he did not recognise, and he was astonished at its intrusion here. He rose up to intercept it—whether it was an unlawful visitor prowling round perhaps to see the handiest way of entry into an unsuspicious house, or some lover bound for a rendezvous, or some servant come out unconscious of observation to take the air. But the new-comer was not afraid of his observation, and he now made out that it was a large old woman in her checked shawl and white cap. Even then Mr. Wedderburn did not recognise the old woman, with whose appearance he was but slightly acquainted. She stopped when they met and made him a slow curtsey, leaning upon a stick. It was too dark for him to see her face.

"Did you want anything with me, my woman?" said Mr. Wedderburn.

"Ay, sir," she said, "I just do that. You'll maybe not know me. I'm Janet Macalister, that was nurse to Mr. Robert D'yell."

"I have often heard of you," said Mr. Wedderburn, "and I am glad to see you, Janet; not that I do see you, for the night's dark. And this is not an hour for you to be out at your years. If you have anything to say to me we would be better in the library or the hall."

"Sir," said Janet, "what I have to say is not for any place where we can be seen. I came out here that naebody might suspect I took such a thing upon me; and yet I'm forced to it—though I canna tell you why."

"This sounds very mysterious," said Mr. Wedderburn; "but I hope there's nothing very wrong."

"Mr. Wedderburn," said Janet, "you're very often at our house."

"Eh!" cried Mr. Wedderburn, in amazement, "at your house? Oh, you mean at Yalton, I suppose. And have you any objections to that?"

"Yes, sir," said Janet firmly, "the greatest of objections. Do you not know, Mr. Wedderburn, that the mistress is still but a young woman (to have such a family), and that she is a widow with naebody to defend her good name—and here are you, a marriageable man, haunting her house every night of your life. Bide a moment, sir, and listen to me. Oh, it's nothing to laugh at—it's just very serious. You are here morning, noon, and night"—(here there was a murmur from the unfortunate man of "No, no! not so bad as that")—"and I ask ye to take your ain sense and judgment to your help and tell me what folk will think that sees that?"

"Think!" faltered Mr. Wedderburn. "Woman, you must have taken leave of your senses. What is it you mean?—and what should they think but that I'm the friend of the family and a very attached one, and that it's my business to be here?"

"Oh, sir, ye'll not content your ain judgment with that, far less the rest of the world! It's no business that brings ye here. Ye come because you're fain and fond to come. I am the oldest person about the house, and it would ill become me to see my bairn's wife put in a wrong position, and never say a word. Sir, the mistress is a bonnie and a pleasant woman."

"I have nothing to say against that."

"And no age to speak of. And you yoursel' what are ye? Comparatively speaking, a young man."

"Comparatively in the furthest sense. I am much obliged to you, Janet."

"Don't think, sir," said Janet, solemnly, "that you can carry it off with a laugh. I will not see the mistress put in a wrong position, and never say a word. It may be want of thought; but you must see, if you consider, that she's not like a young lass to be courted and married. And still less is she one to be made a talk of in all the country side. I will not have my mistress exposed to detractions, and none to the fore to put a stop to them!" said Janet with excitement, striking her staff on the gravel.

Mr. Wedderburn stood, feeling the old woman tower over him with her palsied head and threatening air; he was half angry, half amused, wholly discomfited and startled. The situation was ludicrous, and yet it was embarrassing. To be startled out of the happiness of his thoughts by such an interruption, brought to book by an old servant, warned as it were off the premises by the nurse, was almost too whimsical and absurd a position to be treated as serious; and yet there was an uncomfortable reality at the bottom which he could not elude.

"Janet," he said, "my woman—do you not think you are going a little too far? I was just as often at this house when Robert D'yell himself was here."

"No, Mr. Wedderburn, not half so often."

"Nonsense, woman, much more often! and in any way I am not answerable to you. The last thing I could think of," he added in a troubled tone, "would be to—would be—— You are daft, Janet! I'm their trustee and the nearest of their friends; how dare you say a word about my visits? I will say nothing to your mistress, but I must request you to refrain from such remarks, or else—"

"Sir," cried Janet, "you needna threaten me, for you're not the master here!"

"No, I am not the master here," said Mr. Wedderburn; "but if you think anybody will have encouragement to set up ill stories about—No," he said, checking himself, "I will not blame you with that. You've made a mistake; but no doubt your meaning was good—only never let me hear it any more."

"Oh, sir," cried Janet, "the human heart's an awfu' deceitful thing. I could find it in my heart to go down on my knees, and beg you—oh, for the Lord's sake!—to go away before there's any harm done from this misfortunate house."

"The woman's daft!" cried Mr. Wedderburn.

But it gave him a dazed and troubled look when he appeared in the drawing-room some time later. He was very silent all the rest of the evening, sometimes casting an almost furtive look round him from one face to another; sometimes red, sometimes pale. Once or twice he broke out into a curious laugh when there seemed little occasion for it. "I am afraid you have taken cold, Mr. Wedderburn; it was too late to be sitting out on an October night," said Mrs. Dalyell.

"I don't think I've taken cold—but I think I'll return to my room, with your kind permission, for I have some things to plan out," said the lawyer. It was so unlike him that they all agreed something must be the matter. Had he got bad news? Had he been troubled about business? "Perhaps he had taken something that had disagreed with him," Mrs. Dalyell suggested. Whatever it was, he was not like himself.

No, he was very unlike himself. He gave a shame-faced look in the glass when he went to his room, and burst out into a low, long laugh. "I'm a pretty person!" he said to himself. And then he became suddenly grave—graver, almost, than he had ever been in all his serious life.

CHAPTER VII

It was not until Fred Dalyell's return from Oxford in the spring that he became aware of the rumour which had already begun to spread through the neighbourhood and to be discussed in the Edinburgh drawing-rooms, that his mother was about to marry again. He had seen when he returned home that the girls were a little overcast and subdued, and that there was a little flush as of uneasiness and embarrassment on Mrs. Dalyell's face. It is difficult at first for a long absent member of a family coming back, to find such a cloud in the air, to discover whether this is only the moment of a storm, whether it means some trifling disagreement—for trifles become great in the inclosure of the household walls—or whether something important and fundamental is intimated by these restrained phrases and averted looks. He thought that perhaps there had been a "breeze," that Susie was getting into the wilful stage, and, distracted by hopes and prospects of her own, had been opposing or defying her mother; that the tenants had been troublesome, backward on rent-day, or bothering about those eternal repairs, which he wondered that old Wedderburn could allow to worry his mother. But this did not seem enough to account for the visible but unexplained trouble in the house. When he caught Susie by the arm and drew her aside to ask, "What's the matter?" she shook off his hand with a cry of "Oh, don't ask me, Fred," and escaped from him, leaving him more bewildered than ever. What could it mean? It seemed to the young man that they all avoided him on this first evening of his return. His mother did not call him into her room to ask those minute and repeated questions with which mothers are so apt to tease their boys. "Oh, confound it! Now I am going to be put through my catechism!" he said usually, when he was called to one of these examinations; but its omission gave him a shock which was still more disagreeable. Could it be possible that his mother did not want to see him alone, and that the girls were afraid to be questioned by him? Fred felt very uncomfortable, without the faintest notion what could be the cause of it, when he perceived this constrained condition of the house. Then it suddenly occurred to him that old Pat Wedderburn, as he was generally and profanely called, had not come to meet him as had invariably been the case till now.

"By the by," he cried, "I felt that something was wanting, but I couldn't make out what it was. What has become of old Pat?"

"You should speak a little more respectfully, Fred, of our oldest friend," said his mother reproachfully; but she did not look at him, and the flush grew deeper on her face, which was bent over her work. As for Susie, she pushed her chair away, and almost turned her back upon her mother. Fred immediately divined that old Pat had been objecting to some of Susie's flirtations, which was odd, as Susie was known to be his favourite of all.

"Oh, I'm respectful enough," he said. "I don't mean any harm. The house doesn't seem natural without him. Why isn't he here to-night?"

"He has not been with us quite so much of late," said Mrs. Dalyell, never lifting her eyes from her work; "but he is coming out to-morrow, and he will tell you himself, Fred."

"Has anything gone wrong?" he asked amazed; for the girls, whose voices generally ran chattering through everything, and who on an ordinary occasion would have thrown in half-a-dozen remarks, sat still as two stone images, Susie with her head averted, Alice buried in a book, which she held between her and the light.

"I request," said Mrs. Dalyell, in a voice somewhat high-pitched and imperative, as if she expected to encounter opposition, "that there be no more about it till to-morrow night."

"Oh, if it is me you mean, mamma, you may be sure there will be no more about it—till Doomsday—from me!"

"Susie!" cried her brother in amazement. But Susie's only reply was to burst from the room in a flush of rage and opposition, such as Fred had never seen in his quiet home before. Alice followed her quickly, and the young man thought that now at last there was some chance of having it out. "I suppose," he said, "that old Pat has been at her for flirting—the little pussy that she has grown."

But before he had finished his little speech Mrs. Dalyell, too, had risen from her chair, and, standing with her back to him, was putting her work away.

"You must excuse me," she said, "my dear boy, if I don't enter into it to-night. I'm—a little tired and put out. I must go and look after those girls; and though it's your first night at home, it's late, and I don't think I shall come down again. After your journey, Fred, you should go early to bed."

"After my journey!" he cried with angry dismay. "What has my journey to do with it? But never mind, mother, if you're tired. I'll come to your room, and have a talk over the fire."

"Not to-night," she said, and kissed him. She lingered a moment, patting him on the shoulder with her hand. "I know it must seem strange to you, Fred—but not to-night, not to-night."

As a matter of fact, the least imaginative of lookers-on will allow that the position of a middle-aged mother who has to tell her grown-up son that she is going to marry again must be an embarrassing one. Mrs. Dalyell was not like a girl expecting ecstatic happiness in the union with the man she loves. It was an arrangement which had come to seem natural, partly because she wanted someone to lean upon, and ill-natured gossips (as she heard) objected to that constant, easy, unembarrassing presence of the household friend, which she and her children had found so comfortable—without the existence of some closer bond. She would rather honestly have had Mr. Wedderburn on his old footing; but, if she could not have him on his old footing, it was better to marry him than to lose him. This had been the unimpassioned fashion of Mrs. Dalyell's thoughts. And he wished it. A man, it appeared, even at fifty-seven, could not content himself with the friendship which was quite enough for a woman. Perhaps she was a little flattered to know that this was so, and that in her mature matronhood she still had charms. And she had thought, as he assured her, that it would draw the family bonds closer and make so little difference. The chief difference would be that he would come of right, instead of only for love, and that the interests of her family would be his own, not only much more than his own, as they were at present. It had seemed very plausible, as he set all the advantages forth, which indeed Pat Wedderburn had done, not only to calm her scruples, but also his own; for, had she but known it, he too was very well contented with the existing position of affairs. But if Mrs. Dalyell had known the trouble it would have given her—the wild vexation of the girls, and the horrible necessity of having to tell Fred! No, that last was what she could not do. She had intended to do it on his return, but her courage had failed her. Tell your grown-up son that you are going to marry! No, no, she could not do it. And when two years had not yet elapsed from his father's death! "Oh," she said to herself, "it was no wrong to Robert! Oh, no, no wrong to Robert! It was a different thing, not to be thought of in the same way." But still, when it came to the point, she could not do it, it was beyond her power.

Fred could not tell what to think: he was angry and vexed and cast down by the strange reception he had received. The first night at home, which was always so pleasant, the girls hanging about him with a hundred things to ask and to tell, his mother beaming with affection and pleasure on her united family. And here he was left alone, the lamps burning with a sort of calm intelligence as if they knew all about it, the clock chuckling at him on the mantel-piece. Foggo came in with the tea-tray, and looked round in astonishment for the ladies, then shook his head solemnly and went away, leaving the little silver kettle boiling over its spirit-lamp. Foggo knew too. The very kettle puffed out its steam in Fred's face like a mockery. Everybody knew—except the forlorn young master of the house, who knew nothing, and could not even form a guess what the mystery could be.

He was not however destined to spend that night in uncertainty. As he went upstairs, passing with a sense of injury the closed doors of his mother's and his sisters' rooms, Fred heard himself called in a whisper from the end of the corridor. Had he reflected for a moment he would have known who it must be. But with his mind full of his present trouble he did not reflect; he turned round quickly, hoping to see one of his sisters, and it was not till he found himself in the clutches of old Janet that he recognised the danger of her interference. "Has she told ye, Mr. Fred?" whispered the old woman, approaching her formidable head in the big mutch, and with its little palsied movement, to the young man's face. "Told me what?" he cried with impatience. "Oh, my bonnie lad, dinna lose your temper—you'll have need of all your patience. That she's going to be married upon Pat Wedderburn!"

Fred gave a hoarse cry, which ran along the whole corridor into his mother's closed room, who heard it and trembled—and to Susie's, who sat half desperate over her fire longing for her brother. Not for a moment did Fred doubt the news: it explained everything; but he fled from the creature of ill-omen, the woman who gave it, with a sense of hatred and rage, for which indeed there was no warrant so far as she was concerned. "This is your doing!" he cried with fantastic bitterness. Why should he hate Janet, and how could it be her doing? he asked himself afterwards. But at the moment it seemed to the distracted young man as if this old retainer was one of the Fates, the enemy, not the friend of the house. He would not wait to hear another word, but rushed upstairs and shut himself in his room, as if some evil thing had been at his heels. Married!—his mother, his father's wife, the first authority of his life—the woman without reproach—mamma! With that last baby-cry the cup was filled. The young man flung himself upon his face on his bed. And what an unhappy house it was which the darkness held that night concealed in its outer mantle of peace! Unhappy without any cause, for there was no evil going to be done—no harm: so far as any of these troubled people knew.

Mr. Wedderburn, who came "out" next day with an embarrassment not less than that of Mrs. Dalyell, was roused a little by the desperate self-repression with which Fred received the official announcement. "My boy," he said, "it may vex you that there should be any change, but what we are doing is no wrong to you—nor to any man."

"I have not said it was," said Fred sullenly.

"No, you have not said it was—but you seem to think it's an unpardonable step. It is nothing of the kind," said Mr. Wedderburn, indignant. "The time will come when you will think fit to marry, and then your mother will be turned out of her house; and that will seem the most natural thing in the world. Why should she not have one by her side that will make her comfort his care? Your father would have wished it. She's not a person to stand alone to fight with the world."

"She has her children."

"Her children! Susie, who will have a husband of her own as soon as the lad has enough to live on; and Alice, who will follow her sister's example; and you—when are you here to keep your mother company? A month in the vacations when the house is full—and a marriage whenever it strikes your fancy, with her turned adrift. No, no, my young man! You may not like it, you may scorn both her and me for it. But that face!—as if you were wronged and shamed. Come, come, Fred, that's not an air to put on with an old and faithful friend like me."

"I know you are a faithful friend," cried the young man resentfully. "I never doubted you for a moment."

"But never dreamed that I would push my devotion so far? Well, I have done it, you see. And it's your business, my young man, to make the best of it, and accept what all the powers on earth shall not prevent, I promise you," cried the old lawyer with some heat. There were many people throughout Scotland who were aware that it was not a safe thing to go too far with old Pat Wedderburn.

Mrs. Dalyell, however, insisted upon one thing—that the marriage should not take place until two years after her husband's death, so that there were yet several months of discomfort to get through. However it might end, there could be little doubt that in the meantime an element of extreme discomfort was brought into the house. Mr. Wedderburn, whose happiness had been to spend half the evenings of his life at Yalton, came less frequently and was not happy when he came. Susie had turned into a little firebrand, all the more disdainful and offended by her mother's intentions that she was on the eve of a similar change in her own person. Little Alice swayed from one party to the other, sometimes impertinent, sometimes mournful. The step which was to bring additional happiness in the end (or so it is the conventional necessity to suppose) in the meantime brought nothing but discord, division and doubt, and made the entire party unhappy. How much better, even the two principals secretly thought in their hearts, to have gone on in the old happy routine as things were!

Fred came home again in June after various wanderings, visits here and there. He intended to go away before the marriage, and in the existing state of circumstances to make as short a stay as he could at Yalton, from which his mother meant to remove after this event, leaving the house to be taken possession of by her son. Naturally it was not a very joyful visit: the mother held her domestic place with a kind of unsmiling composure, doing everything as before, ignoring as much as possible the difference in her children's faces; and a little polite conversation went on between those who had been so happily united, and twittered and chattered like the birds a few months before. Mrs. Dalyell would not allow herself to be moved, would not show the impatience which possessed her, kept firm with an immovable steadiness, letting the young ones go and come without remark. It was more difficult for them, who could not ignore her, and whose foolish young hearts were eagerly bent on sending little darts into her, saying things between themselves which she could scarcely resent, yet which went to her heart. And the girls would drag their brother to the other end of the long drawing-room, hanging one on each arm, talking low in his ear, while their mother sat at the table by the lamp, apparently taking no notice. They were very cruel to her, chiefly in ignorance, resenting the fact that she did not mind, and unable to feel any human charity for her, as she sat there isolated, conscious of their conspiracy against her. Mrs. Dalyell's spirit was roused a little by this persecution. She had been doubtful enough of the expediency of what she was about to do from the first, but she became more and more determined to hold to her resolution as they thus united against her: and—what she never thought could have been the case— began to long for the day when she should be delivered from this domestic tyranny and once more breathe freely in an atmosphere where she would not be constrained. Thus it may be supposed there was little comfort one way or another in the troubled house; and it became the order of the day to make the evening as short as possible, to go to bed early, to finish upon any terms, at the earliest moment, the dreary, unattractive evening hours.

Fred was following the little line of ladies with their candles up the stairs, when he was once more stopped, but this time openly, by old Janet. She came to the edge of the great staircase in her nodding mutch and checked shawl. "Will you give me two or three minutes, Mr. Fred," she said.

"For what do you want two or three minutes? I have no time at present," he said quickly, for Susie, who was nearest to him in the procession, had stopped upon the stairs, holding up her candle and looking back upon him. She was like a picture, with her light held up and falling upon her white dress.

"But you must come," said Janet in a shrill whisper. "You must come. Remember what your father said—and this time it's a matter of life and death."

"How do you know what my father said?"

"Ay, that's a question. Come with me, my bonnie man—oh, come with me and you shall know all."

Susie stood like a little light-bearer holding up the candle. "Who are you talking to there, Fred, in the dark?"

"No one," he said, with the prompt unconscious impulse of a child accused.

"No one! Why, it's Janet. Oh, is that all?" said Susie. She lowered her light at once and turned away with the profoundest indifference. The sight of Janet conveyed no sense of excitement or mystery to the girl who saw her every day.

Fred obeyed the old woman sulkily and with the greatest reluctance. He would not have done so at all had not Susie seen her. But he could not show to Susie that he had any reluctance to speak to old Janet, whom the younger members of the family had always held by against all the objections of the younger servants. He went mechanically after her, with a strong return of that resentment which he had felt against his father for the recommendation to consult her. It was grievous to be made to think of that at such a moment, when his father had become more sacred to him than ever, in face of the desecrating change that was about to take place, the injury to that beloved memory. It was the only grievance Fred had against his father. He tried to force it from his mind, to have patience with the old woman as he followed her. She belonged to him. She had been faithful to him all his life. Perhaps she wanted to make sure that she should be provided for when his mother left the place, when Yalton was in his possession alone. Oh, certainly she should be provided for, till her last hour! The only one that was faithful to him. Neither friend nor wife had been faithful to him, but his old nurse was faithful. She was sacred to his son for his sake.

Fred made his heart soft with these thoughts; he overcame his own opposition almost altogether, partly with the sentiment of the nurse's faithfulness, partly with his resentment against the others; and he was ready when he found himself in Janet's room, face to face with her in the light of her lamp, to offer her any assurance of his protection and certainty she might require as to her living and her home. Janet, however, put no question to him on any such score. She shut the door and came up close to him in the lamp-light. "Mr. Fred," she said, "you maun take courage, my bonnie man. There are dreadful things to be said to you to-night. Just summon all your strength and read that."

Fred started at the sight of the paper she put before his eyes. "I see," he said, "it is my father's writing. But you need not show me any letter. He told me himself, the day before he died—"

"Oh, laddie, laddie! take it and read it before I go out o' my senses," Janet cried.

He took the paper into his hands. His father's handwriting, there could be no doubt; but no suspicion of the truth was in Fred's mind. He glanced over it, and thought to himself that he had gone out of his senses, as Janet said, or had lost himself in some incoherent dream. "My wife's marriage must be stopped." What did that mean? A man who died two years ago, how could he write about an event of to-day? Was he going mad? Was he in a dream? Was it some delusion which she had put by witchcraft before his eyes? "My wife's marriage must be stopped." "How could he know?" he asked with blanched lips. "How could he tell there would be a marriage?" He turned upon her a face blank of all expression, pale, in a horror of enlightenment about to come.

"Oh, boy, boy! cannot ye see?" cried Janet. She put forth a long trembling finger and thrust it at the paper, pointing to the date. Fred looked and read. He read it a second time aloud, a strange terror growing upon him: "June 3, 18—." "Why," he said, "why—." Then, stammering and stumbling over the words, broke down. "Why, why," he began again with a laugh, "we cannot all be mad and going to Bedlam! It's this year: June 3, 18—."

The old woman grasped him by both his hands. "It's this year—and we're no mad, though often, often I've felt on the edge of it. We're no mad," she repeated, "and it's this year, and the man that wrote that is in the house this blessed night, Mr. Fred!"

God help the lad! He had but turned his black and terrible countenance upon her, holding the letter helplessly in his hands, when there sounded through the house, cutting the silence like a knife, a sudden wild cry, a shriek, lasting only for a second, but piercing to the heart of the night, to the heart of the house, like some sudden horrible event. It was followed almost immediately after by a rush of muffled feet along the passage: the door was pushed open violently, yet silently, and someone came in like a shot from a pistol, as sudden and unexpected. Fred felt himself shrink towards the wall in his horror and amaze. It was a man who had come in—a man with a beard which covered half his face, yet showed a curious kind of smile coming out of the midst of it, though the eyes were full of an almost tragic seriousness. Fred had fallen back against the wall as this new-comer appeared. The room swam round and round in his eyes, a darkness came over him, he saw nothing for a moment: then slowly came to himself, and saw again, within reach of him, so near that he could have touched him, this man—whom he had never seen before. Oh, could he but have been sure that he had never seen him before! His heart stopped beating—and then with a flutter and a spring went on again, as if it would have leaped out of his breast. The shock of the supernatural, the horror of an awful discovery, came into the young man's brain and almost paralysed it as they clashed together. Ah, had it been but the supernatural! But as that face emerged out of the mist, Fred saw that it was that of a living man—and that he heard it talking—it—as living men do.

"You have told him, Janet?"

"No a moment too soon—just as you were coming. Let the laddie be, let him come to himself. And what was it you were doing? Did she—or you—?"

"I have given her a fright that will put a stop to that," he said, with a strange laugh, hard and harsh: and then he flung himself into a chair, throwing off a dark cloak in which he had been wrapped from head to foot. He added after a moment with a groan, "The way of transgressors is hard!" and hid his face in his hands.

Fred had not moved nor said a word, neither had this strange intruder, save for one glance, taken any notice of him. The young man stood up against the wall, supporting himself by it in a sort of conscious swoon and suspense of being. A moment is like an hour in such a horror of discovery; the idea that was too dreadful to entertain becomes possible, certain, familiar, before you have had time to draw a second breath. His father not dead—not a shameful suicide to cheat the insurance companies as his son had once feared—but a still more shameful survivor, having cheated them, having saved his family and cleared his name by the most dreadful, the most false of frauds, the most tremendous of lies. Fred's whole being surged up like a stormy sea in fierce and violent reaction as soon as he got command again of his stunned faculties—he who had suffered so much misery from the thought that his father had taken his own life in his despair, but who had of late become so tender of his memory, so indignant with those who forgot or were faithless to him! And lo, all his pangs were unnecessary, all his love deceived, and here was the man, living!—a swindler, and a cheat, worse than a bankrupt—having saved his reputation and the comfort of his family by a cheat, the worst of frauds, the most disgraceful. Fred had been ready to defy the world for his father when he came upstairs that evening. He turned now with loathing from the name. Father! What did the word mean?—a cheat, a swindler, the most prodigious and incredible of liars. The youth was hard, as youth is, stern and inexorable. He took nothing into account, neither the motive nor the tremendous sacrifice involved, nor least of all the thought that he himself had profited by this dreadful act. Profited?—he?—Fred? His first act must be to denounce the fraud, to offer restitution. The man should escape first—that he would allow, but no more.

Old Janet came up to him and laid her hand upon his shoulder. "Oh, Mr. Fred, are you not going to say a word to him?—not a word of kindness? Oh, Mr. Fred, your father! that has sacrificed just everything in the world."

"I have no father," said Fred hoarsely. "My father is dead."

The unfortunate man raised his head from his hands, and the familiar eyes, the eyes that had smiled upon the boy's childhood, but which smiled no more, tragic in the misery of a renunciation which was more bitter—but, alas! not honourable like death—turned towards the stern and angry boy with a strange look, not of appeal, but of surprise. The offender knew very well all that was involved to himself in what he had done. He knew that it cut him off as a living man from all knowledge of his family, from all possibility of reunion—that he was dead and worse, so far as old surroundings were concerned; but he was not prepared for his son's stern condemnation. He had anticipated wonder, consternation—but, oh, surely some touch of pleasure in seeing him restored from the dead, some burst of welcome from Fred! He uncovered his face and looked with a ghastly astonishment at the son who thus cast him off without a word.

"Maister Freddie, for God's sake! think what you are saying. Speak a word to him!"

"I have nothing to say," said Fred. "I will make the truth known in a week from this time—if it is the truth. I will be no party to a fraud. I loved my father that died, and his memory, but I can be no party to a fraud. In a week's time—"

The stranger never said a word; he sat gazing with things unutterable in his eyes, wonder above all. His boy! it was cruel, barbarous, inhuman; but—this strange visitor did not condemn the youth. He looked at him with an inconceivable surprise—his boy—Fred! He did not make any protest, but sat up, strangely awakened—wondering: even the object of his visit fading in comparison with this shock for which he was not prepared.

All this time there had been sounds of rushing footsteps and ringing of bells through the house, the commotion of some sudden event breaking into the quiet of the night. And then came a distant sound of Susie's voice, calling: "Fred! Fred!" The young man's heart was rent with passionate emotion, such as he had never known in his life before.

"Nobody must come in here," he said, "to find a stranger in the house. If my mother has been frightened, I will tell her. But not if I can help it. Now, the only thing remaining for me is to make the truth known—when—" He paused. He could not address that dreadful spectre directly; his heart was bitter within him at the man who had thus killed for ever his father's memory, the ideal which he had cherished in his father's name. "When—he has decided what to do."

There was a dreadful pause in Janet's room when the young man went away. Then the stranger said in a musing tone: "So that's what Fred has come to in a couple of years. You see, Janet, you have not been so successful as you thought."

"Oh, my man, oh, my bonnie man! the callant is just distracted with wonder and fear."

"There's more in it than that—and he's right, Janet. We were wrong, you and I. And I must just abide the consequences. I'll lie down on your bed for an hour or two, if you're sure it's safe. And then I'll take the gate. It will be for ever this time, you can tell that boy. I'll neither make nor meddle more; and if he's wise he'll let sleeping dogs lie."

CHAPTER VIII

Robert Dalyell stole forth from the house which was his own, yet could never more be his, in what would have been the dead of night had it been any other season but June and any place but a northern country. It was already daylight, with a pearl-like radiance as of spiritual day, and something more mystic and almost awful in the silence of night, combined with this diffusion of lovely light, than any darkness could have been. He seemed to see the great spreading landscape like a picture, with his own single and solitary figure in it, with a momentary terror of himself alone in that great surrounding silence. He was not afraid of being seen, as he was when he had stolen under cover of the brief darkness into the house; but it occurred to him that anybody who should look out of a curtained window or from the crevice of a closed shutter, and see him walking along at an hour when nobody was abroad, would be afraid of him as an unnatural wanderer in the wide brightness which was night. He was in point of fact a ghost, as he had been believed to be—a man with no place or meaning in the world, with his name upon a funeral tablet, and his place knowing him no more; and like a ghost he passed through the pale diffused light which cast no shadow. Never man was in a position more strange and cruel. He had made the sacrifice of his life, not as his son and his friend had feared, by suicide, but in a more dreadful way. He had put himself to death, and yet he lived. The man had been in this living death for nearly two years. He had lost everything—himself, his name, and his personal identity, as well as wife and children, and home and living. And yet he had never fully realised what it was till now. Something of the Bohemian, something of the adventurer in the man, which had been hidden under the most decorous exterior for nearly fifty years, had made that curious new start in existence almost amusing to him in its absolute novelty and relief from the long monotony of usual life.

Even his sudden going home, with the object of frightening his wife out of a marriage which would have been no marriage, had something of the character of a jest in it. But there was no longer any jest in the matter. He had seen his wife, he had seen his son, and he was at last aware of what it was he had done—the darker aspect of it—the dishonour to others, the deadly extinction of himself, the end of everything which he had accomplished, almost with a light heart. A ghost indeed, offending the eyes and chilling the very soul of those who were most near and dear to him. "A swindler," the boy had said. Was he a swindler? To be sure the insurance offices would never have paid that money had they known; but surely he had paid the price for it. He had died to all intents and purposes. He had given himself for his children—a living sacrifice—not less, but more than if he had really died and been thrown up by the sea, as everybody believed, on Portobello sands. It is hard to see guilt in a transaction, not for your own advantage, for which you have given your life. Robert Dalyell did not blame his son; he could perceive that there was much in what Fred said, though his heart swelled in his breast against that injustice. He was not angry with Fred, but much impressed, and moved (strangely enough) to something like satisfaction by his son's demeanour. The boy was a good boy, wounded in his honour, and therefore inexorable, but only as a good man would wish his boy to be. He was glad Fred was an honourable fellow, feeling it like that. Poor Dalyell himself had all the instincts and habits of mind of an honourable man; he had not seen the dishonour in it; he had thought that, giving his life for it as he had done, there was nothing morally wrong in his act. Surely he had bought the money dear: it was not for him; it was for them, and for their good. There they were, all of them—the wife who was about to give him a successor within two years, and the boy who was himself his successor—safe in Yalton, honoured, respected, enjoying the position to which they were born: while he was an outcast, without anything but what he made for himself, and the boy called him a swindler! He was an honest boy for all that, and Dalyell's mind had a certain forlorn satisfaction in it: though a more forlorn being than he, walking, walking like a ghost through that morning light which began in its pearly paleness to warm to the rising of the sun, could not be. It was wonderful at what leisure he was, in the utter forlornness of his being, to think of them all. He was not sorry that he had given himself to save them. The only thing he was sorry for was that, being dead, he had interfered in it all. He ought to have gone upon his own way—married, too, as he might have done, and got himself new ties in his new life. He believed now that there would have been no harm in that. There would be no harm in it. He would get away as quickly as it was practicable, and get back to his new world, and this time he would feel himself really emancipated. He would think no more of the bonds of the past. She should be free to marry if she liked, and so would he. This old world and he had nothing to do with each other any more.

The foolish thing was that he had come at all on this fool's errand. It was all the old woman's fault. It had been weak of him to let her into his secret, to keep himself up with news of home, to be moved by her horror at this marriage. Why should not she marry if she wished to do so? She had been a good wife to him, and he had made her a widow. He had known that she was not a woman who could act for herself, that she was one who must have a caretaker, a manager of external matters? Why should he interfere with her? It was all that confounded old woman's scruples. But Dalyell decided that he would interfere no more, that he would go back whence he came and marry too, and thus justify his wife. The man's heart was very heavy in his breast when he made this resolution; but yet he had a great courage, and was determined to stand up against fate and get a new life for himself, being thus horribly, hopelessly cut off from the old. The boy would not carry out his threat if he disappeared thus, and was heard of no more. And all would be well with them, all would go right, as he had meant it should when he gave up his life.

By this time the sun had risen, the birds had begun to twitter and hold their morning conversations about all the business of life before it was time to tune up for the concert of the day. Where was he going? He had left such things as he had brought with him at a little lonely wayside public-house near the sea before he went to Yalton, but it was still too early to get admittance there. He found himself on the shore before he knew. Yalton was not above a few miles from the sea, or rather from the Firth in its upper part, not far from the spot where that monstrous prodigy of science, about which so many trumpets have been blown, the Forth Bridge, now strides hideous across the lovely inlet—those golden gates through which the westering sun was wont to stream unbroken from the upper reaches of the great estuary upon the stronger tides below. Dalyell came out upon it suddenly, forgetting in the intense preoccupation of his thoughts where he was. The sun had risen beyond the distant Grampians, touching the Fife villages all along the coast with gold. The air was damp, yet sweet with the saltness of the sea in it, and the breath of distance and the sensation of the vast unknown to which this great, splendid ocean pathway was one of the ways. When Dalyell came out thus upon the shore he was the one speck of animated being in the whole still world. He sat down to rest for a little upon a rock. At three o'clock in the morning there is nothing stirring, not even the cattle, though they were waking and thinking of an early breakfast in the fields. He sat there and noted, and thought over it all again. He was very forlorn, but not angry with anybody, scarcely vexed by the thought that he was so soon forgotten. He even laughed a little at the thought of Pat Wedderburn. How had he got himself the length of that idea of marrying? He divined old Pat's thoughts, a little troubled by the necessity, going bravely through it. He had no sense of resentment towards any of them. As soon as there was any one stirring about the "Dun Cow" he would steal in and get his things and some breakfast, and take himself off at once and for ever—never, whatever happened, to interfere again.

But in the meantime there was some time to wait, and the sun was growing warmer every moment, and the tide was in, and the little wavelets rippling along the shore. Baths were not luxuries known at the "Dun Cow," and here was the bath he liked best, ready before him. It would be the last time he would ever bathe in his native waters. He slipped out of his clothes, laid them in a little heap, without even thinking how on one supreme occasion he had done that before, and plunging from the nearest rock launched himself into the sea and sunshine. It would brace him up for the journeys and troubles of the day.

Dalyell swam about for some time, and dived and sported in the water like a boy, with a curious sudden lightness of heart. He could not make up his mind to come out of the water. And the northern seas are cold at three o'clock (getting on for four) in the morning, with the sun not yet very strong, and but newly risen. What it was that happened there was no one to tell. Perhaps it was the shock of the night's proceedings, though he had reasoned it away, which struck to his heart—perhaps it was the cold of the water—it might be a cramp, which, had there been any one near to help, would have been of little consequence. None of these things would any one ever know. It was said afterwards that a cry was heard, piercing the sober stillness of the morning, so that somebody woke and got up at the "Dun Cow," but finding no sign of harm, went to bed again for another hour. And it is certainly true that the minister woke in his manse, which is near the shore, and got up and opened his window, and remarked upon the beauty of the morning, and the wonderful delightful calm and brightness of the Firth. He thought after that it must have been the drowning man's cry that woke him, though he was not conscious of the sound itself.

Thus, with the strangest repetition, all the incidents of Dalyell's fictitious drowning were reproduced; and it did not fail to be remarked in the papers that the accident up the Firth was singularly like the accident that had happened nearly two years before to Mr. Dalyell, of Yalton, on Portobello sands. It was a remarkable coincidence: but the sufferer in this case, it was added, was a stranger, who had arrived at the "Dun Cow" the night before, and was supposed to be a foreigner. The body was found among the rocks, as if he had made a despairing grip upon the seaweeds that covered them to save himself, from which it was judged that the misadventure was wholly accidental; but, naturally, all was conjecture, and this was a thing that never could be known.

CHAPTER IX

Fred went to his mother's room, about which an agitated crowd had already gathered, the two girls and their maid, and an anxious domestic or two from downstairs, besides Mrs. Dalyell's own maid, who was with her mistress. Foggo stood outside on the staircase, anxious to know if he should go for the doctor, and still more anxious to know what had happened, for there was already a conviction in the house that it was not mere illness which had produced that shriek which startled everybody. Mrs. Dalyell was not the kind of woman to shriek from physical pain, and there had been a whisper in the house that the horseman had been heard in the avenue, which, naturally, was a preparation for trouble. Fred, however, was not admitted till some time later, of which the poor young fellow was glad: for he was in no condition to meet his mother in the nervous and excited state in which she must be, while he himself was so shaken and miserable from the same cause. He went to his own room and endeavoured there to calm himself, and thrust away the appalling question that was now before him. How lately he had said to himself that his father's previsions had all been mistaken, and instead of having to take upon himself the anxieties and cares of the head of the house, to break off his studies and turn his thoughts to the grave side of life, he had only been more free, more independent, than before, since he had succeeded his father as Dalyell of Yalton. Ah! but who could have thought of this, this further chapter of disaster, unimaginable, incurable, which would involve the name of Dalyell of Yalton in dishonour and shame— the name his ancestors had borne in credit and pride, the name that poverty and ruin could not have stained, but which must now perish amid records of deceit and fraud. Fred's very heart seemed to shrink and wither up within him when he thought of what he had now to do. It would be his to put the stamp of shame upon that name—to expose the whole disgraceful story, the dishonest means by which downfall had been staved off, only to fall more dreadfully upon the unhappy and innocent now. No, he must not palter with right and wrong, he must not allow any sentiment of pity either for the criminal or for himself to steal in. The criminal! Now that Fred had time to think, that criminal—whose very name he could not endure to think of—whom he had denounced and disowned with such force and almost hatred—had looked at him, oh, with such fatherly eyes! He had scarcely said anything, not a word in his own defence. Fred felt that if he had stayed another minute his courage would have failed him, and the old dear familiar image would have regained its power. The criminal!—worse than a fraudulent bankrupt, almost worse than a suicide, and yet so like—oh, so like—! Oh, he must not think, he must not allow himself to fail in his duty. In a week's time—that was what he had said—to give full time for that fugitive to escape, that he might not be taken or injured, or brought to justice. In a week's time! There must be no paltering with duty. It was clear before him what he had to do.

And then there began to pluck as it were at the skirts of Fred's mind thoughts of what this thing was, of what it must have cost. Had not the man died, had he not more than died? It was not suicide, but it was worse. He had given his life while still a living man. Strange words crept into Fred's mind, which did not come there of themselves, as if some one had thrown them into the surging sea of passion and pain which was within him. Greater love hath no man than this. Oh, silence, silence! these words were said of another, a greater—one Divine. Greater love hath no man than this: they came back and back: as if they could be applied to a man who was a sinner, who had committed a fraud, and deceived his fellow men! Had he deceived them? Had he not died? Died more terribly, more completely than the man in the family grave in Yalton churchyard, who was not Robert Dalyell. Which would one choose if one had to choose? Surely the home in the churchyard, the tablet on the wall—and not the life of an outcast, the death in life of a man who had no identity, who had neither name nor fame. Fred's young soul was rent asunder by these thoughts. There had been no relenting in him, no pity. But now outraged nature avenged herself. Oh, how cruel he had been, how harsh!—not a word of kindness in him, not a softening touch. And he ought not to think of nature now, he ought not to be moved by kindness. He ought to subdue all relenting. In a week's time! He must set his face like brass. He must think of nothing that could make him fail.

It was late when Fred was called to his mother, and he went down as timid as a child called to an interview of which it knows nothing, but that it must involve terrific consequences. He had looked at himself anxiously in the glass before he obeyed the summons, wishing that he knew some way of making himself look less pale, his eyes less excited. The girls knew ways of doing this, Fred believed, but he did not know. He plunged his head into cold water to relieve the heaviness and heat he felt, as of something bursting from his forehead; and then he went downstairs, slowly labouring to collect his thoughts to think what he should say. Mrs. Dalyell was in bed, her head with the background of the red curtains looking at the first glance almost ghastly, her face very pale, her eyes excited like his own. She grasped him by both hands and made him sit down by her. The candles were still burning, but a faint glimmer of blue showed between the curtains. She kept holding his hand, but it was a minute or two before she spoke.

"Fred, do you know if I said anything? What did I say? What did they tell you? Did they say that I—?" She gasped for breath, and could not finish the sentence, but did so with her eyes and with the pressure of her hand.

"I heard nothing, mother, but that you fainted."

She pressed his hand tightly again and said, "I didn't faint. I let them think so—to conceal—Though I was scarcely conscious of what I was doing, I felt it gleam through me that to let them think I was unconscious was best. But I never was unconscious for a moment, Fred—you understand what I am saying?—nor was I asleep, nor could I have been dreaming. You hear what I am saying, Fred?"

"Yes, mother: but don't, for heaven's sake, excite yourself; it may make you ill again."

"What will make me ill? I want you to understand. I've not been ill, only—that they might have no suspicion. Fred, above all things I want you to understand that I am in my full senses, meaning every word I say."

"Yes, mother," he said, pressing her hand.

She renewed her grip upon it, as if she were holding fast to something lest she should be carried away. "Well!" she said, with a long-drawn breath. Then looking him full in the eyes as if to defy misunderstanding: "Fred," she said, "I have seen your father!"

"Mother!" he cried.

"Hush—this was what I was afraid of—that you would think me out of my senses. Look at me. I am not calm, perhaps, but I am as steady as you are." (That was not saying much; but absorbed in her own extraordinary sensations, Mrs. Dalyell fortunately did not notice Fred.) "I was not thinking of him, nor even questioning as I sometimes do. I was more quiet than usual: when, just there, where the curtain is, I saw your father!"

"You must have been over-excited, mother, though you did not know it. My coming home and the girls' talk—and all of us making ourselves disagreeable—without knowing it your mind must have—"

"My mind was quite calm. I made allowance for you children. I could have sympathised with you. But don't go away with any such idea. I saw your father—as plain as I ever saw him in my life."

What could Fred say? He patted her hand to soothe her, and shook his head gently; he could not trust himself to speak.

"It all passed in a moment," she went on. "He said something. I feel sure he used the word marriage, but I was too much startled to make out, and I was so foolish as to give that cry. I can't tell you what a dreadful feeling came upon me. I am not a woman to scream, but I could not help it. And he disappeared, and they all came rushing in."

"It must have been an optical illusion, mother—that's what they call those sort of things. You were disturbed by all of us, and your imagination got excited."

"Don't speak such nonsense to me. I saw your father as I see you. Fred, that's not half I've got to tell you." She closed her fingers more and more closely upon his hand, and drew him close to her. "He was changed," she said almost in a whisper. "He was not as he used to be." She put her face nearer to her son's. "An apparition would have been nothing in comparison. It would have been not wonderful, considering everything. But this: Fred"—she drew him quite close and her fingers were upon his hand like iron—"Fred, your father had grown a beard!"

"Mother!" he cried again.

"You think I'm mad, and I don't wonder: but there's more in what I say than you think, Fred: a man who was dead could not do that. Fred, find me words. I don't know what to say. There is more in this than we know."

They looked at each other, the eyes of the one shooting light and meaning into those of the other. How could the boy stand the keen scrutiny of his mother's eyes? He faltered before her and tried to avert them, but failed. At last he faltered, "Mother! I think your guess is right!"

She seized him by the shoulder with her other hand and shook him in the vehemence of her passion. "Have you known this all along? Have you known and never said a word?"

"No," he said; "how could you think it? Could I have been a party to a fraud? But I saw him too—to-night."

Mrs. Dalyell's hands relaxed; she fell back upon her pillow, and, covering her face with her hands, began to cry and moan. "Oh, how shall I ever look him in the face! How shall I ever look him in the face!"

Fred was prepared for many things on his mother's part. He was prepared to see her burst into indignation like his own; he could have understood her stern and angry, or he could have understood her grieved and miserable. He could even have understood it—had she been unreasonably and foolishly glad. But ashamed, asking how she could look him in the face!—this was beyond the knowledge of her son. After a little she calmed down and said with the echo of a sob, "We will have something to forgive each other—on both sides."

"Mother," cried Fred, "do you realise all the difference it will make?"

She was silent for a moment, with a flush upon her face. "Oh, my dear," she cried, with a look of awe, "how can we ever be sufficiently thankful that we knew in time!"

This was all she could think of, it seemed; and poor young Fred had to return to his own troubled thoughts by himself without help from his mother. She entertained, it would seem, no doubt as to her duty towards her husband. The fraud did not weigh on her mind. He had come back—that was all.

CHAPTER X

In the afternoon of the miserable day which had begun in this wise, Fred was sitting alone, trying to come to some conclusion in the crowd of his unhappy thoughts. His mother had been able to rest after her agitation, and sleep, but had sent for him again early to ask for his father—where he was in the meantime, and when he was coming home? It had better, she thought, be got over as quietly as possible, and all the friends informed. Mr. Wedderburn was always fond of Robert: he would take it very quietly; he would see that the less said the better for all parties. Her mind was full of these thoughts. She had arranged everything in her mind. There would be much to forgive—on both sides—which perhaps on the whole was better than had it been entirely on one. As for business matters, Mrs. Dalyell was aware there must be troubles; but fortunately this was not her share of the business. Robert and Mr. Wedderburn would settle these things. It all seemed so simple as she put it, that Fred withdrew again with a sort of artificial calm in his spirit, but had no sooner been alone for ten minutes than the hurlyburly began over again. What was he to do? Inform the insurance companies? But what could be done to raise the necessary money? Throw Yalton into the market—or what? Anyhow, it must be ruin, whether the father came home or disappeared again; anyhow, his own happy career was over, and nothing but trouble was to come.

In the meantime he did not know where his father was, or what had become of him, and he had not yet the courage to question Janet, who no doubt knew. Janet was at the bottom of it all. For all he could tell, it might be she who had first suggested that dreadful expedient out of which all this misery came. Oh! had the family been but ruined honestly, naturally, two years ago! Fred felt, like a child, that it must be that wretched old woman's fault all through, and he could not subdue his mind to the extent of asking her for information. It would come, he felt sure, in good time.

And so it did: that afternoon Foggo entered the library where his young master was sitting, with a very mysterious air, and informed him that there was "one" who desired to speak with him. Fred's heart leapt to his mouth, for his thoughts were bent solely on his father, and it seemed certain that it could be no other than he.

"A gentleman," he added faintly, "with a beard?" It was the only description he could venture upon.

"No, Mr. Fred, not a gentleman at all—John Saunderson from the 'Dun Cow.'"

"John Saunderson from the 'Dun Cow'?"

"It was to speak about something that had happened. He said that if the young laird would have the kindness to step out at the gate—he's no just in trim for a grand house, and he would like to speak to yourself in a private way."

"Bring him here, then, Foggo."

"No, Mr. Fred: he would take it far kinder if you would just step out to the gate."

And this was what Fred finally did. He found the landlord of the "Dun Cow" exceedingly embarrassed, not knowing how to begin his story. He took off his blue bonnet at the sight of Fred, and began to twirl it round and round in his hands.

"It's about an accident that's happened," said John.

"Do you want me to do anything? I'm very much occupied; if it's anything Foggo could do—"

"Na, it's not Foggo I want" (he said Foggy, after the fashion of his locality), "it's just yoursel'. There was a gentleman came to lodge in my house last night. We whiles get a stranger—that's not very particular."

"A gentleman?"

"A gentleman with a beard." The man eyed Fred very closely, who did not know what to reply.

"Yes," he said, with a little catch of his breath, "and what then?"

"The gentleman must have gone down, so far as we can see, very early to take a bath in the sea. Nobody heard him go out. My own idea is he never was in after he got his supper. He first went to the door for a smoke, and my impression is—"

"What happened?" said Fred. His mouth was so dry he could scarcely speak.

"He must have gone into the sea to take a bath awfu' early in the morning, before we were up. The wife she thought she heard a cry about four o'clock, and I got up, for she gave me no peace, and looked about and saw nothing. But later there was one came running and said a man's clo'es were on the sands, close by some rocks—just for all the world as they were that time, ye mind, Mr. D'yell, when your father was lost. I just took to my heels and ran all the way to the sands. And there was his clo'es, sure enough."

"The man?" Fred gasped again.

"They got him after a bittie, with his hands clasped full of the seaweed, and his knee raised up upon a rock. He must have made a fight, poor gentleman, for his life. Na, I see what you are thinking: it was nae suicide. He had got up his knee upon a bit of rock, and his hands were full of the weeds—nasty slimy unprofitable things." There was a pause, and the man lowered his voice a little significantly before he said, "I would like much, Mr. Frederick, if you would come down and see him."

Fred was not able to speak. He shrank more than he could say from this dreadful sight. He shook his head in the impulse of his panic and horror.

"Sir," said the man, "I've known your father, Mr. Robert D'yell, Yalton, man and boy, for more than forty year. If I didna know he had been drowned two years ago I would say yon was him."

It was with difficulty Fred found his voice: "I think that I know who it was. It was a—near relation."

"Ah, I can well believe that," said John Saunderson. He was something of a genealogist himself, as so many people of his class are in country life, and he threw a hasty backward glance over the scions of the house of Yalton, which he had known all his life, and settled within himself that there was no such near relation, no cousin that ever he had heard of. He did not say this, nor his own profound conviction as to the drowned man.

"A man," said Fred, "that we had thought to be dead—for years. He frightened my mother with the likeness you speak of, and I am afraid he did not get a good reception. Oh, Saunderson, you are sure it was not a suicide?"

"So far as I could judge—no. I am not surprised," said Saunderson, "that the mistress was terrified. It gave me a kind of a shock. 'Lord bless me,' I said, and then I just held my peace, for I would not be one to raise a scandal on the house of Yalton. But my ostler, confound him, has a long tongue."

"I'm much obliged to you," said Fred. "I'll come down."

And there he saw, on the poor bed in the "Dun Cow," surrounded by the few rustic houses about, all excited and discussing the tragedy, his father, at last hushed and safe, seized by the death which he had cheated once, but could not cheat a second time. The dreadful drowning look had departed from his face; he lay tranquil and calm, like a man who had died in his bed, who had never wronged either man or woman. Whom had he wronged? Perhaps the insurance companies—no one else. And Fred at length came to the conclusion that there was now no occasion to disturb the insurance companies. It had come to pass at last—the event which had been supposed to be accomplished long ago. There was no reason now for the confession he had intended, no need to expose his father's deception, to betray the secret of the house. Fred could scarcely reconcile himself to the fact that this was so. It cost him a great deal of trouble to make up his mind that his business now—now that all was over, and his father gone for ever—was to be silent for ever. Mr. Wedderburn had been summoned, and this was his advice, as well as the almost imperious command of Fred's mother. To throw a stain upon her husband's name was intolerable to Mrs. Dalyell—to attract attention to the house and explain its secret history. She said, with tears, yet with indignation, that it should not, it must not be. And old Pat Wedderburn, who was strangely moved by the story, and who said not a word in blame of his friend, supported her strongly. "They would have had to give the money now, if not then," he said, "and it's not your part to open the question. Let it alone. Let him rest in his grave at last—poor Bob! And I hope in my presence no one will ever say an ill word of Bob D'yell."

There was a tear in the old lawyer's eye. Perhaps he understood it best of the three, though the other two were wife and son. Fred's statement that the drowned man was a relation made it possible to lay him in the Yalton vault after all—his last and rightful home. Who the other was, who had received that sad hospitality in the name of Robert Dalyell of Yalton, they never knew, nor was it necessary to inquire.

Somehow, however, there was no more question of Mrs. Dalyell's marriage. Neither bride or bridegroom ever spoke of it again. And Mr. Wedderburn resumed something of the old easy relations after a while, and presided at Susie's marriage, and was the best friend of the house, as he had always been. It was a conclusion which on the whole they all felt to be the best.

Margaret Oliphant – A Short Biography

Margaret Oliphant Wilson was born on April 4th, 1828 to Francis W. Wilson, a clerk, and Margaret Oliphant, at Wallyford, near Musselburgh, East Lothian.

She spent her childhood at Lasswade, near Dalkeith, Glasgow before moving to Liverpool.

Her youth was spent in establishing a writing style so much so that, in 1849, she had her first novel published: Passages in the Life of Mrs. Margaret Maitland based on the Scottish Free Church movement. It met with some success and was a good start to her career.

Two years later, in 1851, her third book Caleb Field was published. It was also now that she met the publisher William Blackwood in Edinburgh and was asked to contribute to his well-received Blackwood's Magazine. It was to be a lifetimes endeavor. Over the course of the relationship she would have well over 100 articles published.

In May 1852, Margaret married her cousin, Frank Wilson Oliphant, at Birkenhead, and they settled at Harrington Square, Camden, London. He was an artist working primarily in stained glass. With the marriage she became Margaret Oliphant Wilson Oliphant.

Their marriage produced six children but three tragically died in infancy.

When her husband developed signs of the dreaded consumption (tuberculosis) they moved, on the advice of doctors, to warmer climes. In January 1859 it was to Florence, and then to Rome where, sadly, he died.

Margaret was naturally devastated but was also now left without support and only her income from her writing. She returned to England and took up the task of supporting her three remaining children by her literary activity.

By now she was being published both as an established novelist and regularly in Blackwood's Magazine, amongst others. Her incredible and prolific work rate increased both her commercial reputation and the size of her reading audience.

Against this her domestic life continued to be tragic, full of sorrow and disappointment.

In January 1864 her only remaining daughter Maggie died and was buried in her father's grave in Rome. Her brother, who had emigrated to Canada, was shortly afterwards involved in financial ruin. Margaret generously offered a home to him and his children, adding another demand to her already heavy responsibilities.

In 1866 she settled at Windsor to be closer to her sons, who were being educated at near-by Eton School. That year, her second cousin, Annie Louisa Walker, came to live with her as a companion-housekeeper. Windsor was now to be her home for the rest of her life.

Her literary career for three decades was one of constant delivery and success. Whether she wrote historical works or across several genres in fiction: domestic realism, historical, romance or supernatural she was successful.

For more than thirty years she pursued a varied literary career but family life continued to bring problems.

The literary ambitions she wished for her sons were unfulfilled. Cyril Francis, the eldest, died in 1890, leaving a Life of Alfred de Musset, incorporated in his mother's Foreign Classics for English Readers. The younger, Francis, who she nicknamed 'Cecco', collaborated with her in the Victorian Age of English Literature and won a position at the British Museum, but was rejected by Sir Andrew Clark, a famous physician. Cecco died in 1894.

With the last of her children now lost to her, she had but little further interest in life. Her health steadily and inexorably declined.

Margaret Oliphant Wilson Oliphant died at the age of 69 in Wimbledon on 20th June 1897. She is buried in Eton beside her sons.

At her death, Margaret was still working on Annals of a Publishing House, a record of Blackwood's Magazine with which she had enjoyed such a successful relationship.

Her Autobiography and Letters, which present a thoughtful picture of her domestic anxieties, was published in 1899. Only parts were written with a wider audience in mind: she had originally intended the Autobiography for her son, but he died before she could finish it.

Opinions on Oliphant's work are split, with some critics seeing her as a 'domestic novelist', while others recognize her work as influential and important to the Victorian literature canon. Critical reception from her contemporaries is also divided. John Skelton took the view that Oliphant wrote too much and too quickly. Writing a Blackwood's article called 'A Little Chat About Mrs. Oliphant', he asked, "Had Mrs. Oliphant concentrated her powers, what might she not have done? We might have had another Charlotte Brontë or another George Eliot." However not all of the contemporary reception was negative. The esteemed M. R. James admired Oliphant's supernatural fiction, concluding that "the religious ghost story, as it may be called, was never done better than by Mrs. Oliphant in 'The Open Door' and 'A Beleaguered City'. Mary Butts lavished praise on Oliphant's ghost story 'The Library Window', describing it as "one masterpiece of sober loveliness".

More modern critics of Oliphant's work include Virginia Woolf, who asked in Three Guineas whether Oliphant's autobiography does not lead the reader "to deplore the fact that Mrs. Oliphant sold her brain, her very admirable brain, prostituted her culture and enslaved her intellectual liberty in order that she might earn her living and educate her children."

Whatever the merits of their cases Margaret Oliphant has been shamefully neglected in modern years. She is now becoming more widely recognised as a leading writer of her day.

A canon of more than 120 works, including novels, travel books, histories, and volumes of literary criticism.

Novels

Margaret Maitland (1849)
Merkland (1850)
Caleb Field (1851)
John Drayton (1851)
Adam Graeme (1852)
The Melvilles (1852)
Katie Stewart (1852)
Harry Muir (1853)
Ailieford (1853)
The Quiet Heart (1854)
Magdalen Hepburn (1854)
Zaidee (1855)
Lilliesleaf (1855)
Christian Melville (1855)
The Athelings (1857)
The Days of My Life (1857)
Orphans (1858)
The Laird of Norlaw (1858)
Agnes Hopetoun's Schools and Holidays (1859)
Lucy Crofton (1860)
The House on the Moor (1861)
The Last of the Mortimers (1862)
Heart and Cross (1863)
Salem Chapel (1863)
The Rector (1863)
Doctor's Family (1863)
The Perpetual Curate (1864)
Miss Marjoribanks (1866)
Phoebe Junior (1876)
A Son of the Soil (1865)
Agnes (1866)
Madonna Mary (1867)
Brownlows (1868)
The Minister's Wife (1869)
The Three Brothers (1870)
John: A Love Story (1870)
Squire Arden (1871)
At his Gates (1872)

Ombra (1872

May (1873)

Innocent (1873)

The Story of Valentine and his Brother (1875)

A Rose in June (1874)

For Love and Life (1874)

Whiteladies (1875)

An Odd Couple (1875)

The Curate in Charge (1876)

Carità (1877)

Young Musgrave (1877)

Mrs. Arthur (1877)

The Primrose Path (1878)

Within the Precincts (1879)

The Fugitives (1879)

A Beleaguered City (1879)

The Greatest Heiress in England (1880)

He That Will Not When He May (1880)

In Trust (1881)

Harry Joscelyn (1881)

Lady Jane (1882)

A Little Pilgrim in the Unseen (1882)

The Lady Lindores (1883)

Sir Tom (1883)

Hester (1883)

It Was a Lover and his Lass (1883)

The Lady's Walk (1883)

The Wizard's Son (1884)

Madam (1884)

The Prodigals and their Inheritance (1885)

Oliver's Bride (1885)

A Country Gentleman and his Family (1886)

A House Divided Against Itself (1886)

Effie Ogilvie (1886)

A Poor Gentleman (1886)

The Son of his Father (1886)

Joyce (1888)

Cousin Mary (1888)

The Land of Darkness (1888)

Lady Car (1889)

Kirsteen (1890)

The Mystery of Mrs. Biencarrow (1890)

Sons and Daughters (1890)

The Railway Man and his Children (1891)

The Heir Presumptive and the Heir Apparent (1891)

The Marriage of Elinor (1891)

Janet (1891)

The Cuckoo in the Nest (1892)

Diana Trelawny (1892)
The Sorceress (1893)
A House in Bloomsbury (1894)
Sir Robert's Fortune (1894)
Who Was Lost and is Found (1894)
Lady William (1894)
Two Strangers (1895)
Old Mr. Tredgold (1895)
The Unjust Steward (1896)
The Ways of Life (1897)

Short stories
Neighbours on the Green (1889)
A Widow's Tale and Other Stories (1898)
That Little Cutty (1898)
The Open Door (1918)

Selected Articles

Mary Russel Mitford (Blackwood's Magazine, Vol. 75, 1854)
Evelin and Pepys (Blackwood's Magazine, Vol. 76, 1854)
The Holy Land (Blackwood's Magazine, Vol. 76, 1854)
Mr. Thackeray and his Novels (Blackwood's Magazine, Vol. 77, 1855)
Bulwer (Blackwood's Magazine, Vol. 77, 1855)
Charles Dickens (Blackwood's Magazine, Vol. 77, 1855)
Modern Novelists—Great and Small (Blackwood's Magazine, Vol. 77, 1855)
Modern Light Literature: Poetry (Blackwood's Magazine, Vol. 79, 1856)
Religion in Common Life (Blackwood's Magazine, Vol. 79, 1856)
Sydney Smith (Blackwood's Magazine, Vol. 79, 1856)
The Laws Concerning Women (Blackwood's Magazine, Vol. 79, 1856)
The Art of Caviling (Blackwood's Magazine, Vol. 80, 1856)
Béranger (Blackwood's Magazine, Vol. 83, 1858)
The Condition of Women (Blackwood's Magazine, Vol. 83, 1858)
The Missionary Explorer (Blackwood's Magazine, Vol. 83, 1858)
Religious Memoirs (Blackwood's Magazine, Vol. 83, 1858)
Social Science (Blackwood's Magazine, Vol. 88, 1860)
Scotland and her Accusers (Blackwood's Magazine, Vol. 90, 1861)
The Chronicles of Carlingford (Blackwood's Magazine 1862–1865)
Girolamo Savonarola (Blackwood's Magazine, Vol. 93, 1863)
The Life of Jesus (Blackwood's Magazine, Vol. 96, 1864)
Giacomo Leopardi (Blackwood's Magazine, Vol. 98, 1865)
The Great Unrepresented (Blackwood's Magazine, Vol. 100, 1866)
Mill on the Subjection of Women (The Edinburgh Review, Vol. 130, 1869)
The Opium-Eater (Blackwood's Magazine, Vol. 122, 1877)
Russian and Nihilism in the Novels of I. Tourgeniéf (Blackwood's Magazine, Vol. 127, 1880)
School and College (Blackwood's Magazine, Vol. 128, 1880)

The Grievances of Women (Fraser's Magazine, New Series, Vol. 21, 1880)
Mrs. Carlyle (The Contemporary Review, Vol. 43, May 1883)
The Ethics of Biography (The Contemporary Review, July 1883)
Victor Hugo (The Contemporary Review, Vol. 48, July/December 1885)
A Venetian Dynasty (The Contemporary Review, Vol. 50, August 1886)
Laurence Oliphant (Blackwood's Magazine, Vol. 145, 1889)
Tennyson (Blackwood's Magazine, Vol. 152, 1892)
Addison, the Humorist (Century Magazine, Vol. 48, 1894)
The Anti-Marriage League (Blackwood's Magazine, Vol. 159, 1896)

Biographies

Edward Irving (1862)
Francis of Assisi (1871)
Count de Montalembert (1872)
Dante (1877)
Cervantes (1880)
Life of Sheridan in the English Men of Letters series (1883)
John Tulloch (1888)
Laurence Oliphant (1892)

Historical & Critical Works

Historical Sketches of the Reign of George II (1869)
The Makers of Florence (1876)
A Literary History of England from 1760 to 1825 (1882)
The Makers of Venice (1887)
Royal Edinburgh (1890)
Jerusalem (1891)
The Makers of Modern Rome (1895)
William Blackwood and his Sons (1897)
The Sisters Brontë. In: Women Novelists of Queen Victoria's Reign (1897)